WE'LL GROW ORANGES
IN ALASKA

Allison Nicole Gentry

*For my grandmother, Jane Gabler, my parents Jim &
Christine Gentry and my 7th grade English teacher*

We are all searching for meaning within ourselves, that we've re-stricted and ruled out a parallel of lifelines in hopes of fitting in or avoiding lonliness. We're told and we even believe that we have one agenda, one pre-determined destiny to fulfill. Am I attracted to you because of the circumstances or the contrary?

PREFACE

The first time she saw him, she knew right away that there was something different about him. He wasn't like all the other students. There was a certain distinction to him. Something overlooked—something most teachers hadn't had the eyes to recognize. In fact, most people missed it actually. Or perhaps they were just too tired from all their years of professional service and daily grind to see past their routines. But Ellie was different. She had a chip on her shoulder. She always had to be the savior on account of her personal shortcomings. She was so convinced and motivated that she would be the one to help him, she couldn't see that she was the one who really needed to be saved. Loris would be, to both their surprise--her saving grace in spite of her personal shortcomings.

It started out like any other school day in the bustling city of Hong Kong. Children were rushing in, flooding the school's gates. Teachers sighed, muttering among themselves that Friday was just another few days away and Chinese New Year was just around the corner when in fact it was a few months away. This banter always started on a Monday and continued until the last bell rang on Friday afternoon. The school bell sounded and tardy pupils were kept behind in order to not disrupt the morning assembly while the rest of the students lined up by class. The disciplinary master made her way towards the stage.

"Good morning, students," she said sternly as if talking to a group of prisoners in a concentration camp. Her eyes darted, glaring out, challenging someone to try and disrespect her just so punishment could be carried out. She got off on punishment.

"Good morning, Mrs. Green," the students said monotonously, with sleep still in their eyes.

Not satisfied, she snapped back, "Let us try that again, shall we? Good morning, students." Her eyes narrowed even more. It was a wonder she could even see.

"GOOD MORNING, Mrs. Green," they all said bowing, eyes wide opened now. Hong Kong students were groomed at the early age of four to show the utmost respect to their teachers.

Still dissatisfied, Mrs. Green opened her mouth to speak but stopped herself when she took out her gleaming pocket watch and realized the time. She snapped her mouth shut and recomposed herself. If there was anything to know about Mrs. Green, it was that the only one thing more important to her than respect was punctuality—a characteristic she regarded in the highest of standards, not just with her pupils, but also to all other subordinates especially her teaching staff. Everyone feared her—more so the teachers than the students since there was more at stake for them. The only way to get on Mrs. Green's good side was to beat her at a game of poker and everyone knew that was her game. Lose, and not only will you have lost your money, but you will have wasted her time, and she would never let you forget it. You would become indebted in more than one way.

"As you all know, Mrs. Butler is no longer with us as she is now on maternity leave," she said clenching up her face as if the thought of it disgusted her. She detested children and thought babies were the worst kind of children. The students let out a sign of instant approval, making it clear that they would not be missing their replaceable English teacher.

Ignoring them, she continued. "So, without further delay, I

would like you all to welcome your new English Literature teacher, Ellie," she said motioning for the new teacher to come on stage. As the new teacher approached the podium, the room instantly fell silent and everyone's eyes darted towards her, trying to size her up. Some showed instant approval while others, mostly the teaching staff, weren't so impressed. She looked way too casual and young to be a teacher and the turnaround rate for English teachers at this school was high due to student discipline problems. It was only a matter of time until she too had enough and quit. They wouldn't waste their time investing in getting to know her. Sensing that she was now the focus of attention, she drew in a deep breath and approached, trying to appear confident though she was really trembling inside. Handing her the mic, Mrs. Green urged her on.

"Good morning, everyone! My name is Ellie, but I guess you already knew that," she said, letting out a nervous laugh; her hand holding the mic shook uncontrollably. Still silence. "I'm really excited to be at your school and hope I am able to get to know each and every one of you personally. I'll be hosting a fun English activity at lunchtime in the Multi-purpose Room today for those of you who are interested in coming to get to know me! Hope to see you all there!" she said handing the mic back to Mrs. Green and scurrying away in her high heels as fast as possible, being careful not to trip on her way out.

"I expect you all will not give Ellie any trouble and will welcome her with open arms," Mrs. Green said carefully eyeing the pupils, knowing full well that they would certainly be causing the same trouble that they had given Mrs. Butler forcing her to take early maternity leave when her baby wasn't due for another few months.

CHAPTER 1

As the first-period bell rang, Ellie had already been in her classroom preparing for her first lesson with her Form 6 students. She wanted to start off by doing a few ice-breakers with them to show her class that she was the fun and cool teacher. This was the first of many mistakes she would make. Standing in front of her desk, she eagerly waited for her students to arrive, but as they started trickling in, she was not met with the same enthusiasm as she had hoped.

"Where should we sit, Miss?" one sleepy-eyed boy asked, without making eye contact.

"Oh, I didn't plan on giving any of you assigned seats, so just have a seat anywhere you like," she replied energetically. Without acknowledging what she had said, the boy headed towards the back of the classroom, slumped into a chair and promptly fell asleep. As the other students made their way in, Ellie remained optimistic.

"Good morning, class," she said facing the students. All but the sleepy-eyed boy stood up. "Good morning, Missy," they said in unison as if they were all under the same drowsy spell.

"Please, call me Ellie," she said with a big smile. "As you all know, I'm here to teach you all about English Literature, but today, I would like to spend our class time getting to know all of you! So, I prepared some ice breakers we can play," she said grabbing for the papers she so diligently spent preparing late the night before. Letting out a loud sigh of disapproval, one girl disengaged and took out her mobile phone and started texting, not even trying to be discreet.

"Phones away, dear," she said making her way to the girl. "Come on, phones away," Ellie demanded, now standing in front of the girl trying to get her attention.

"It's a waste of time honestly, Miss. You're just going to leave like all the rest," the sleepy-eyed boy woke up to say staring straight at her now. Turning her attention to him, she smiled, but this time it wasn't as enthusiastic as before.

"What do you mean— like the rest?" Ellie asked trying to fully understand why there was clearly some bad blood between her and the students she had literally just met. "What's your name?" she asked.

"Loris," he said staring at her with no emotion.

"Well, Loris, you'll find I'm different from most teachers," she said turning to the whole class. She would prove to them that she was different, that she did care. A challenge she gladly accepted. She thought it wouldn't be hard to do.

"How about you start then, Loris? The game is called 'Two Truths and a Lie.' You start by telling your classmates three things about yourself—two true things and one lie. Afterwards, we get to guess which one you are lying about. Simple enough right?" Ellie said thinking about how much fun this game could be.

"If it will get you to stop talking about how you're different than other teachers, then ok," Loris said sighing as his classmates laughed.

Mrs. Abrams leaned on Loris' desk and watched him walk towards the front of the room to address the class.

As he was passing by, he gave her the once-over, not even trying to hide his wandering eyes while Ellie tried to pretend she didn't notice, but her face gave her away.

He smirked, seeing her flushed cheeks. "It's cute when you get embarrassed, Miss," he muttered as he passed by. He said it just loud enough for her to hear.

"Alright, the first thing is that I'm a virgin," he said looking straight at Ellie. The whole class roared out in laughter. Clearly there was something Ellie hadn't known. She was starting to regret not setting rules for her game of choice. "The second thing is that I help my dad at his auto shop on the weekends and the last thing is," he said pausing for a bit, "I want to fuck you Miss," he said grinning at Ellie as if she was the only person in the room.

The whole class exploded in commotion, laughing at Loris' response. Trying to keep her cool, Ellie tried to calm the class down. "Alright, alright Loris, be appropriate. Now give us one more thing," she said now avoiding his eyes. She was determined for this game to be a success. She wasn't going to back down so easily.

"Can you guess which one is the lie Miss?" he said, still trying to catch her attention.

"You're definitely a virgin Loris!" one prissy girl shouted out.

"You're just jealous he didn't want to fuck you," another came back with. "The last one is clearly the lie! Who would want to fuck you Missy?" she said, her words cutting like knives. Secondary school girls had become a lot meaner than she remembered.

"Any other takers?" he said confidently, opening up his arms. The whole class starting chanting virgin, virgin! Afraid she had lost not only the game but the class' respect as well, Ellie tried to change the topic.

"Alright stop! Let's give someone else a go, shall we?" she said motioning him back to his seat.

"In case you're wondering Miss, the second one is the lie, my dad doesn't have an auto shop," he said winking as he returned to his seat and disappeared behind his school bag to sleep.

"Alright, who's next?" she said scanning the room. She would have moved on, but she was confident her ice breaker would be a hit and wasn't about to admit failure. "How about you sweetie? What's your name?" she said approaching a student she thought wouldn't be any trouble.

"Cherry," she said coolly.

"Ok, Cherry, tell us three things about yourself. Two truths and one lie."

"You first Miss. I think you should demonstrate what is and isn't appropriate information to share," she challenged.

"You're right. Let me give you an example," she said missing the sarcasm in Cherry's voice.

"So, the first thing is that I'm married.

"BORING!" one student shouted out.

Ignoring them, she continued. "The second is that I'm forty years old and the last thing is that I love metal music. Alright, who would like to guess? Cherry?"

"Number 1! There's no way you're married, Miss, or you'd be wearing a ring, isn't it?" she said rolling her eyes.

"Ok, anyone else want to guess?" Ellie said desperately searching the room for volunteers. *I'd have a better chance of finding a tribute for the Hunger Games than a volunteer in this class*, she thought. She probably would have volunteered as tribute herself if it meant she would be rescued from this classroom.

"The second one, obviously," a boy shouted out.

"Well done!" Ellie said applauding.

"Your tits wouldn't be so perky if you were forty," he finished. And there it was.

"OK! Enough! Why would you say something so awful and to

your teacher," she said slamming her hand on the nearest desk, but the strike wasn't as powerful as she would have liked. She felt angry for being so angry; they were just students. They didn't really hate her; they were just taking their anger out on her because it was easier than facing their own demons. She hated having so many excuses and logic for defending bad behavior.

"Ok, I don't know how your old English teacher was and what she did or did not allow, but let me assure you that saying those things to your teacher is not acceptable. Understood?" she said searching for understanding in her pupils' eyes.

"I said, understood!?"

With a bit of hesitation, the class slowly nodded their heads but eye contact was scattered.

"Ok, let's try something different then. One by one, please stand up and tell me your name and something interesting about yourself. I'll start. My name is Ellie and I've written and published two books before. Next? Let's start with you," she said pointing to Cherry.

"I'm Cherry and I play volleyball," she said quickly sitting down.

"Volleyball, nice, next?"

As the last student had finished, Ellie lightened back up. She wasn't used to being the strict teacher but she was realizing she just might have to be to survive in this school and to protect her heart. She always got too invested and involved in her work. There was no shut off button for her and it drove her husband mad.

"See, that wasn't so hard, was it?" she said trying but failing to get a smile from her students. "Now, I'll be handing out your new literature booklets that I have compiled myself. You'll find this booklet is not like the traditional literature books you've had before but contains a wider variety of reading texts. Please write your name and class number and turn to the first page.

You'll see the class syllabus and everything we will be doing for the rest of the semester. Are there any questions?"

One student slowly raised his hand. "Yes?"

"It's Felix. Yeah, it says that two students will be teaching and presenting in class for each lesson?"

"Yes, and...?"

"Well, isn't it the teachers job to teach us and not the students?" he said. His classmates quietly backed him up.

"Ah, good question Felix. As you'll come to learn, I have a different approach to teaching. I believe you will all learn better if you are given more responsibility for your learning." Sitting on her desk, she continued, "So, starting next week, we'll be talking about 'Romeo and Juliet.' Two students, whom I will choose, will present to the class about this topic and lead a class discussion. The guidelines are in the first few pages of your booklet. So, if you're still unsure of what to do, you can always find me. Now, for the rest of the lesson, I want you guys to get into groups of two and discuss which topic you are interested in presenting and let me know before the end of class."

The rest of the lesson passed on with minor interruptions as most students were or at least appeared to be on task. All but one—Loris. Walking to the back of the class, Ellie went to wake him up when the bell rang. Students immediately began to pour out of their seats and out of class, paying no mind to the proper goodbyes they would usually say to their teachers marking the end of a lesson. Ellie was too distracted or perhaps too defeated to enforce it on the first day. Besides, she was preoccupied with Loris.

Loris raised his head and saw his teacher hovering over him.

"That's a bit creepy, Miss," he said getting out of his seat.

"Are you like this with all your teachers?" Ellie asked boldly, crossing her arms.

"Like what?" he smiled and left before Ellie could reply. She was certain he knew what she meant.

CHAPTER 2

As the rest of her lessons flew by without major setbacks, Ellie returned to the staffroom desperate for another round of coffee.

"So, how's your first day going?" a husky, well-put-together man asked in a cheeky British accent as he approached the water cooler. She could sense the small talk coming. There was no escape.

"As well as can be expected, I guess," Ellie replied, taking small sips of her coffee, unable to forget the words of the confrontational student from her first lesson. "Well, there is one student who is giving me a bit of a struggle. His name's Loris from…"

"Oh, him" the man said cutting her off. His tone changed immediately. "Don't mind him love. He's a lost cause and always causing trouble. He's one of the reasons Mrs. Butler left, if not the only one."

"I thought she was on maternity leave?" Ellie asked confused.

"Yeah, but that shouldn't have been for another few months or so, and she isn't coming back here after. So just put the pieces together, love."

She was growing annoyed with his frequent use of the word love. She knew it was common in Britain but they were in Hong Kong and no matter how much time he had spent overseas, he should have known calling someone love here was highly inappropriate as he was local guy. They had just met after all. He needed to dial back the charm and disrespect.

"I see. Well, what's his story? Do you have any advice for how I can help him?"

"There is no helping that boy. Best just ride it out until he eventually drops out. The school board just needs one more slip up from him, and then the boy is gone."

"Is it possible to meet his mother or father and have a talk with them?" Ellie asked. She really was a go-getter. First day and already asking to talk to the parents. A rare gem indeed. Also, a foolish one.

"Good luck getting them on the phone," the man said grabbing a yogurt out of the fridge. "He lives with his dad who isn't much use," he started imitating chugging a bottle. "And his mum ran off with some young hot piece. Haven't heard from her since."

"So, what should I do then?"

"Just leave him alone. Save yourself the trouble love. Focus your energy on other students who will appreciate your efforts. We can only do so much," he said walking towards his cubicle.

Forget about him? The words kept ringing in Ellie ear. She wanted to make sense of the conversation that had just happened. How could another teacher say something so negative about a student? How could he be so nonchalant about a student's wellbeing and future? *He'll probably be kicked out soon anyways? Wasn't it a teacher's job to try their best to prevent this from happening?* Taking the last gulp of her creamy coffee, she slammed the cup down and made herself a promise. She would help this student even if he rejected her and it made her job as well as her life a living hell for the time being. After all, everything is temporary and this, too, will pass. She was certain.

Leaving school after the first day had been long anticipated. Ellie quickly tidied up her desk, threw on her beanie, and wrapped her scarf around her body before making her way out. Blending into the sea of students wearing their heavy winter gear, she became unrecognizable. She placed her earphones in and put on her favorite playlist of metal. The closest train was about a ten-minute walk and, having taken a taxi this morning, she didn't know the way. She figured she would follow the rest of the crowd, as most students would obviously be heading there. Or at least walk far enough to see the signs pointing to the nearest MTR.

"Woah, check out the ass on her!" one boy shouted out to his mates. Figuring they were talking about another student, Ellie turned back to see what they were all gawking at only to realize that all three boys' eyes were plastered on hers. Horror filled two of the boy's eyes when they realized it was not another student but their teacher.

"Shit, do you think she heard us?" one of the boys said to his friend.

Turning back around, Ellie quickened her pace, pretending to not have heard the boy's remarks. It was after school hours and she didn't even know what she could have said in reply. She squeezed her headphones in tighter. Obviously embarrassed, the three boys raced past her and caught up with their other mates, when one decided to look back. It was Loris.

"See you tomorrow, Miss," he said winking, making it clear that he knew she had heard everything that had just happened. Burying her face in her scarf, she prayed for the weekend to come.

CHAPTER 3

When she got home, she sprawled out onto the couch without even taking off her shoes. She was exhausted. She turned to look at the office door and saw light escaping from under the door. Her husband was home. The anxiety of thinking of what to eat for dinner crept in and further ruined her melancholy mood. She'd just lay there for another twenty minutes before taking on the daunting task of decision.

"Rough day? Didn't even bother to take your shoes off? Are we that lazy?" her husband appeared from his office that she never went in.

"Sorry, I just had a long day."

Her husband ignored her hint at a plea for reassurance and cut straight to the chase.

"So, what's for dinner?"

Her eyes narrowed. "Uh, I hadn't really thought about that to be honest. Maybe we can do take out? I'm pretty tired."

"Forget it, I'm going out, then with the boys. I thought we would have a nice meal for once, but if you're too tired, I'm just going to meet some mates for drinks."

"No, I can cook, I just need some time," she said getting up.

"Forget it. You know one of the reasons I got married was because I thought I wouldn't have to worry about things like this, but apparently that's just out the door," he said grabbing his keys and wallet. He slammed the door behind him.

Great! Just what she needed. On top of angsty and emotional teenagers, she now had a man-child to deal with. She couldn't be bothered.

"Take out it is then." She changed out of her teacher clothes into something more comfortable and headed out. She knew exactly where she was going. McDonalds.

Her husband refused to eat there and said it was one of the reasons his sexual attraction towards her had dwindled. "Maybe if you stopped putting crap in your body," he had said, "you wouldn't look so gross. It's hard to look at you sometimes." Making love in the dark, if you could even call it that, had become the norm. She hated him for it.

The closest McDonald's had been shut down for renovations, so she went to the next one a stop over. She couldn't wait to order her big mac, extra-large curly fries, and strawberry shake; hell she even considered adding in a few pieces of chicken nuggets. She deserved it.

"Can I help you," a familiar voice said. The boy was staring straight at the register. His hat covered his face.

"Yeah, a big mac, extra-large curly fries, large strawberry shake, and two 6-packs of chicken nuggets."

He looked up immediately, also recognizing her voice.

"Ellie?"

"Loris? I didn't know you worked here."

"Why would you, you just met me today. It'd be kind of creepy if you knew." There was his sense of humor again.

"Yeah, that's true; just a habit to say that, I guess."

"Is this all for you?" he said referring to her order.

"So, what if it is?"

"Hard day?"

"You were there."

He laughed. "Yeah, I'm sorry about that. Anyways, you don't need to worry about me, ok? I can take care of myself."

"I don't doubt it. Do you want to talk about it?"

"Save yourself the trouble. I won't be in school much longer," he said handing her the order.

"I wish it was that easy, but I can't change who I am."

He looked around, "I'm a bit busy right now," she turned and saw the massive line that had formed behind her.

"I can wait if you want to talk."

"I don't get off till 12."

"On a school night? How often do you work?"

"Five or six days a week, depending."

"No wonder you're having so much trouble at school."

"Listen, it's nice you care but like I said, I'm fine. It's not your problem."

"You sure you don't want me to wait?"

"Don't you need to get back to your husband?"

"No."

He squinted his eyes and furrowed his brow. His mouth twisted up. His face was full of curiosity. "Alright then."

She waited in the lobby for a few hours until all the customers started to clear out and Loris had finished his shift. She devoured her food and kept checking her phone. No missed calls. Her husband was still out.

"Alright, you ready?" Loris asked approaching her.

"Ready for what?"

"I'm starving. Unlike you, I didn't just eat a family meal."

"Hey!"

"I'm just joking. Come on," he said leading her out.

They walked to an outdoor dim sum place and an old woman greeted Loris instantly. They seemed familiar. She motioned for them to sit down and brought them green tea and a bunch of steamed dishes. *Loris must be a regular here*, she thought.

"Do you like Dim Sum?"

"I love it, especially the BBQ pork buns and radish cakes."

"We got those both here," he said passing her the dish.

"Oh, I couldn't; I'm still full."

"Really?" He could see through her ruse.

"Alright, just a little." She took a bite into the BBQ pork bun, and it was the best one she had ever had. "Wow!"

"It's good, isn't it? You can't find better dim sum."

"Damn. How'd you find this place?"

"I've been coming here since I was little."

"That's a nice tradition."

"It was."

There was something curious about his answer, but she didn't want to push.

"Do you want to walk around for a bit?" he asked.

"Sure."

They made their way to the park and started walking on one of the foot trails. It was usually so overcrowded with people that you couldn't see the actual trail but it was deserted at this time, except for a few streetlights that lit up the path. They found a bench and sat down in Lai Chi Kok Park.

"Can I ask what you meant when you said you won't be in school much longer?"

"I meant exactly what I said."

"Can you explain? If you plan on leaving, why not just do it now; why stretch it out?"

"If it was that easy, I would have left a long time ago, but my dad... he won't let me."

"Is that why you're trying to get kicked out?"

"Who told you that?"

"No one... just... when I mentioned your name to one of the teachers, they said.."

"Why were you talking about me?"

"No, not like that, I just wanted to help you, to understand you."

"And let me guess, they said don't bother?"

She was quiet.

"Typical. I bet they can't wait until they can kick me out. I bet they'll throw a party once it's done," he raised his voice.

"Don't say that!"

"It's true, isn't it? None of the teachers at that school give two shits about me."

"I care."

"Why? Why should I believe that?"

"Because it's true. Because I'm with you right now at 1am on a school night."

His face softened. "Too bad I didn't meet you earlier. Maybe things would have turned out differently."

"They still can. It's not too late."

"I wish I believed that."

"You have to fight. Don't give up and let them be right."

"I don't care about them being right or what they think."

"I know, but you have to keep trying."

"It's no use. Even if I try, they just see what they want. Disappointment. Failure."

"I don't see any of those things. Do you know what I see?"

He sighed, "What?"

"I see someone with so much potential. Someone who has been disappointed and let down one too many times. Someone who needs someone to believe in them."

"And that's you?"

"I want it to be."

He took out a cigarette and lit it up. "You going to tell me not to smoke?"

"No, I was going to ask for one," she said reaching out her hand.

"Huh," he snickered. "Hard day for both of us."

"I'm sorry you've been let down, Loris, but I really do want to help." She grabbed his hand and squeezed.

He misread the intention. He turned his hand, so it was now in hers and held it tightly. She didn't pull away but sat there perplexed, taking a long drag from her cigarette. Maybe this was his way of accepting her help. Maybe he needed this.

"You're already helping," he said turning closer to her. She could feel his breath on her face.

"Good, we'll figure this out," she said looking ahead. They were still holding hands. She started to open her hand, but Loris clamped tightly.

"Loris..." she said looking at their hands now.

"Ellie, I.." he leaned in and tried to kiss her. She stood up horrified and backed away.

"What are you doing?!"

"Trying to kiss you. What does it look like?" he said getting up, about to try again.

"I'm your teacher, Loris!"

"I don't care about that. We can be together; no one has to know. It'll be our secret."

"Stop! I'm sorry if you misunderstood me. I do care about you, but not like that."

"You're right, I don't understand. You just spent half the night leading me on, and now you're saying it's not like that? I don't get it." He stood and stormed off.

"Wait," she chased after him and grabbed his arm. He tried to jerk free, but she pulled him back and hugged him tight. "I do care about you Loris, and I'm going to do everything I can to help you. Please don't give up on yourself like everyone else. Let me help you."

He surrendered to her embrace for about ten minutes without talking. Everything was silent around them except for their heart beats that were off the charts.

"I'm sorry," he said, finally pulling away. "I didn't mean to disrespect you. I know you care. I just am not used to anyone being nice to me; it's usually because they want something or are into me that way. My bad."

"It's ok. You don't need to apologize."

"Yes, I do. It was wrong. I'm sorry."

"Thanks. Listen it's getting late; we should be getting back home. It's only a few hours till school starts."

"Ugh, don't remind me."

"See you tomorrow," she said giving him one last smile for the night. She felt good going home knowing he was willing to let her help.

CHAPTER 4

As the months passed, the students seemed to be warming up to Ellie. And to her advantage, some even started to view her as the fun teacher who cared. Loris was still being a bit difficult in terms of motivation, but he refrained from his inappropriate comments and was at school. So that was a start. The shift in students' behavior, however, caused several of her colleagues to resent her. The religious affairs teacher, Ms. Peng, thought that Ellie was too lax and friendly with her students and that this was no way to behave. It set a bad precedent. In her defense, she believed that all students learned best by discipline and, if given too much freedom, would tarnish their character and succumb to temptations brought on by the devil himself. It was a teacher's duty to teach strong moral character, she felt.

Another English teacher, Mr. Kwok, felt vindictive towards Ellie when some of his students complained that they wished they could be in her class. These "office politics," however, didn't seem to bother her. As long as the students were happy and learning, that was all she needed. It wasn't a competition. What did she care if a bunch of bitter, middle-aged teachers had it out for her? They didn't respect their own titles and it was clear as day, even to the students, that they didn't give two shits about the students or what they were teaching. It was and always had been about the money. It was no wonder students like Loris acted out the way they did. They didn't have anyone who believed in or encouraged them. Instead they had a bunch of hypocrites preaching "the good word."

One sunny afternoon though, the growing resentment of her colleagues had finally reached its tipping point. One bold colleague had finally decided to move on from the office gossip and mustered up the courage to lodge a formal complaint against Ellie. This led to her getting an invitation, if you could call it that from the office admin to speak to Mrs. Green. Knocking on the firm oak door, Ellie took a deep breath in before entering. She had always been afraid of going to the principal's office as a student, and this fear didn't seem to escape her even after graduation.

"Come in," a flat voice beckoned.

This couldn't be good.

"You wanted to see me, Mrs. Green?" she said politely.

"Have a seat." Ellie watched her take out a forty-year-old scotch from the bookshelf behind her and pour herself a glass. Not offering Ellie any, she assumed this was not going to be a friendly visit, it was a power play. In any other circumstance, it'd be frowned upon, even illegal to bring alcohol on school grounds, but Mrs. Green was the exception. No one dared challenge her. She was set in her ways and was in a much more forgiving mood when she had a drink.

Mrs. Green crossed her legs and took a long sip, leaving no traces of her dictator purple lipstick on her glass. El wondered how she did that.

"I've been getting complaints from some of your colleagues that you've been being a bit too friendly with your students."

Just then, the image of her holding Loris' hand to comfort him popped up. But there was no way this was about that.

"Too friendly? I'm sorry, but how is that a complaint?" Ellie said getting defensive.

Ellie could see Mrs. Green's upper lip start to twitch. She puckered up her face like she had just tasted something sour and not to her liking. She repositioned herself on her chair and started to drop names

"I heard from Ms. Peng that you do not discipline your students properly during lessons and that your teaching style is rather lax," she said, raising her eyebrows. "Care to explain?"

"I assure you, Mrs. Green, my teaching style is anything but lax. Maybe it is more progressive, but I truly believe the students are really benefiting from it. I think the teachers here could learn a thing or two from watching a class." Mrs. Green bit the inside of her mouth and swirled her tongue along the top of her teeth.

"And Mr. Kwok tells me that you are more of a friend to the students than a teacher. He even said you have your students teaching lessons? Now what's that about?" she said taking another long sip. Ellie stared at the empty glass and waited for her to top it up before explaining herself.

"It's called flipping the classroom, where the teacher becomes the student and the students become the teacher. It's a great way for them to learn essential life skills as well as learn that their opinions matter," Ellie said sticking strongly to her beliefs.

"So, you're letting the students do your job then?"

"No, not at all. Maybe I'm not explaining it well. Let me try to say it another way," she said getting flustered. It was hard to educate someone who was already set in their ways.

"Don't bother. Just stop doing what you're doing and get back to doing your actual job, the one we hired you to do," Mrs. Green said standing up and looking towards the door.

Realizing there was no winning or reasoning, Ellie surrendered temporarily and apologized. She left the room, frustrated at having a new enemy. She wasn't about to just let it go and laugh with her colleagues who had just betrayed her. She was out for blood, and it was personal. It was one thing to insult her personally, but to insult her teaching was a whole new level.

Leaving the principal's office, she rushed out, bumping into a student along the way. "Getting in trouble, are we?"

She didn't have to look up to realize who it was. "I hope you're not," she said giving him the look.

"Don't worry, I've been good," he said relaxing back into his seat. "I hope so," Ellie said.

"Just here for my weekly check-in. They want to see me crack. But don't worry, I won't give them the satisfaction," he winked.

"Good. You don't need that."

"Exactly. Who needs them when I have you and all of your support?" Loris said punching her shoulder like a mate. "See you in class Monday," he said as Mrs. Green called him in.

Ellie wondered if Mrs. Green would put the whisky away or just carry on.

CHAPTER 5

I t was finally the weekend. Ellie threw down her bag full of dictation and composition corrections and immediately went for the glass of wine that had been calling her name all day before hopping in the shower.

Throwing back her head and closing her eyes, she let out a deep breath and opened her mouth to let the water in. Her whole body ached from the stress and pressures of teaching, but the hot water was helping a bit. Her husband had left on a business trip for a few days and wasn't going to be back till later tonight, so she would be able to have a personal night and not have to worry about whatever the hell he'd think of to complain about. It was always something.

As she ran the showerhead over her body, she drifted back into thinking about work and her student Loris. Hundreds of random questions popped into her mind. Had he always been like this? Was he hardworking and motivated until his mother left? When did it start? Was there really no other teacher who saw potential in him? Did he mean everything he said about her being attractive and wanting to fuck her or was he just being cheeky? She thought she had him figured out, especially after they had a heart-to-heart, but she still couldn't help but wonder.

Did he have a girlfriend? Of course not, otherwise he wouldn't have tried to kiss her? She got so preoccupied with all the questions about who he was that she didn't realize the showerhead, now between her legs, had switched to the pulsating setting. The pressure growing stronger and stronger until she couldn't take it anymore and surrendered, releasing all of the pressure that had been building up inside. Letting out a long sigh of relief and coming back to reality, she realized what had just happened. Had she just gotten off while thinking of her student? What a silly thing to think. The two actions had just happened at the same time. There was no correlation between the two. But if that were true, why was she feeling incredibly guilty about it. She had just showered but somehow still felt dirty. Trying to brush it off, she threw on her silky robe, grabbed the bottle of wine she had been airing, and plopped down in front of the TV to watch reruns of her favorite guilty pleasure, The L Word. She didn't have the mental energy to start a new show and ignored her phone that had been lighting up since she got home; she was in no mood to socialize with anyone, including her husband who was doing who-knows-what during his trip. To her, this was the perfect way to spend a night. Alone.

Passed out on the couch with an empty bottle of wine in her hand, she woke herself up to the sound of the wine bottle crashing onto the floor. Smash. Looking at the clock, she noticed it was 3am and her husband still wasn't back. This behavior was typical, but normally he would always call her if he was planning on being late or something came up. Glancing at her phone, she just saw the twenty-something messages from her friend Clara pressing her to go out with her that night to the docks, which was the place to be on a Friday night. Full of bars and food trucks, people often went there to drink and chill on the piers while watching the boats light up the harbor as they sailed by.

Pushing all doubts aside, she got up and went to her bedroom and noticed her husband's black loafers on the mat next to the door. Oh, so the bastard was home after all. Crawling into bed, careful not to wake him up, she positioned herself towards the wall, clutching her favorite stuffed animal she had ever since she was a child.

"Drinking again, Ellie?" her husband said, pulling her closer to him.

"I missed you," she said trying to cuddle. He pulled her close, but it wasn't in the comforting way she had hoped.

"Show me how much you missed me," he said pulling down his boxers and forcing his way inside of her mouth, making her do all the work. She pulled back, she wasn't in the mood, but her husband pushed himself back in, moaning out and ignoring her body language.

"Faster, faster," he said grunting. "Show me how much you missed me, you slut," he said pulling her hair back as she yelped out.

Turning around to kiss her husband, he rejected her advance and whilst avoiding eye contact shoved her head down back to pleasure him. She wondered if he was thinking about her while she went down on him. She became insecure and gave her all, stroking his tip with her fingers and licking the skin below his balls rapidly with her darting tongue, but his mind seemed to wander elsewhere. He was somewhere else. He then commanded her to go lower with his hands, ignoring her objection, while she used both hands to masturbate him and forced her face between his cheeks. She was inside of him, using her tongue to penetrate him rapidly. Then, without warning, he started clenching up and moaning loudly like a man who lost control and came all over her face. He pushed her aside instantly without even a thank you or a good job or a kiss.

"Go clean yourself up," he said rolling over, going back to sleep.

"Can I have a kiss?" she said pleading, trying to prove to herself that her husband still loved her. What she had done for him was out of love. She would never have considered doing this for anyone else before, but he had pressured her by saying she needed to meet his needs, or he would find someone who could.

Her husband had already passed out or at least pretended to be when his wife called out for attention in one last attempt.

Poor Ellie, still in denial, wasn't ready to face the fact that her husband was just not that into her anymore and that the only reason they were still together was because he just didn't have the energy or money to get divorced at the moment. He just couldn't be bothered. She was a convenience. She was a toy.

CHAPTER 6

Rolling into the school parking lot on the following Monday, Ellie had taken a taxi again. It was becoming a daily routine. She would wake up late, miss the bus, and then frantically wait around for a red taxi to pass by. She would do her makeup on the way. Wearing makeup made her feel invincible. Without it, she could barely get through a day of teaching.

Hopping out of the taxi, she heard the first bell warning her to hurry up. She made her way towards the school entrance when she noticed Loris smoking in the alley that joined the two schools. Still slightly embarrassed about what had happened Friday night, she debated whether or not she should intervene. But she knew if another teacher spotted him, he'd have hell to pay.

"Loris, put that out," Ellie said giving him a warning.

He looked at her and took one long puff.

Ellie grabbed the lit cigarette from his mouth and accidentally brushed her fingers against his lips. She chucked it to the ground and stomped it out with her heel in anger.

"Do that again, Miss," he said looking straight into her eyes with curiosity.

Turning red, she lashed out, asserting her authority. "There won't be a next time Loris, do you hear? Not if you get caught."

She grabbed him by the arm and escorted him to the entrance. Teachers normally were discouraged to make physical contact with students, but she felt this was an appropriate situation for force. She had to make sure he wouldn't be late to class. He was already on thin ice and was pushing his luck. Something must have happened over the weekend to make him behave so defiantly.

"They're so soft," he said running his fingers over his lips, mimicking what she had just done. He watched her reaction carefully.

Ignoring his advances, she turned to him right before entering school.

"Don't do that," Ellie said pleading with him.

"Do what, Miss?"

"You know what," she said giving him that look every student dreaded. She knew it was a self-defense mechanism, but he had to find other ways to deal.

About to take another jab, he stopped suddenly. "I'm sorry. I didn't mean to."

Her face softened, it seemed like he was genuine.

"It's just you're so beautiful, I can't help it." And there it was again.

She sighed, letting go of his arm she had been holding.

"Well, you need to try," she said walking away, pretending nothing had just happened. It was better that way. Loris already had enough problems. Adding sexual harassment of a teacher to his list of misdemeanors would certainly give the principal the ammunition she needed to finally expel him and probably Ellie as well. There were only two more months of school till graduation, and Ellie was determined for Loris to be there for graduation. She wasn't about to cave.

"'Atonement.' A book famous for deceit and betrayal of a familiar kind," Ellie said closing the book. "Peter and Coby will be your teachers for today's lesson. So, let's get to it, shall we? I know you all read the book as it was your homework for the past week, so the rest of you should be thinking about some questions you have for your discussion afterwards," she said with great enthusiasm. This was one of her all-time favorite reads. As the two students spoke of love, misunderstanding, assumptions and betrayal, Ellie listened intently, becoming unaware of the other students in the class. As expected, most students hadn't done the reading assignment. Ellie expected as much, but what she hadn't expected was what came afterwards.

"So, the moral of the story is that you shouldn't assume you know everything, especially if it has nothing to do with you," Coby said. "It's not your business. Unless you are absolutely sure of what happened, it is best to let it go," Coby sat.

Ellie stood with a nod of approval. It wasn't the best analysis, but it was clear they had tried their best. "Well done, Coby and Peter. I think we've all learned a lot." Turning to the rest of the class, she saw that no one else seemed to be as impressed as she.

"Well, come on guys! Thoughts? Opinions? Questions to get us started with discussion?" she said hoping there was at least one student in the room who was moved by the book. Looking around, one voice spoke out.

"Don't you think her punishment isn't enough?" a judgmental voice chimed.

Looking back, she saw it was Loris. Not the sleepy-eyed boy she had first encountered, Loris engaged in class for the first time.

"Whose punishment? You mean the little sister's?" Ellie prodded.

"I mean she accuses this man of raping her sister and friend and with what proof? Because she is rich, she is automatically trusted? And then, despite everything, her sister's plea for the man's innocence, he is thrown in jail and left to rot—ruining two lives," he said with growing anger in his voice as if it were personal.

"Well, the book is called 'Atonement,' another student piped in, "and written from her point of view. You don't think it's enough that she regrets her actions? She was only a child; she couldn't have known the consequences of her actions."

"Oh! She knew what she was doing. Why wouldn't she ask her sister first if she thought he was hurting her?" Loris said defending his position.

"Good to see so much energy for this. Now let me ask you," Elllie said calming the rumble of discussions down. "How many of you think the younger sister was able to atone for her actions?"

Most of the class raised their hands.

"And how many of you believe that it all came a little too late? There was no going back, the damage was done?"

Loris remained still. "What do you think, Miss?" Loris asked as the whole class turned towards Ellie.

"Well, I've always considered myself a romantic, and this story deeply moves me. Although I believe the younger sister is sincere in being sorry and regrets her actions, I do believe it all came a little too late. Because of her false accusation, her sister and lover were never able to have the happy ending they deserve, and that's quite tragic really. Even more tragic than Romeo and Juliet I would say," Ellie said getting lost in thought.

The bell rang jarring Ellie from her daydream and reminding her that she was still in front of the class. She snapped back, realizing most students' attention had already wandered—all, but one's. Watching as her students exited the classroom, she noticed that Loris had stayed behind, taking extra time tidying up his books.

"Miss," he said approaching Ellie.

"Yes, Loris? What is it?" she said hoping something inappropriate wasn't going to be the next thing coming out of his mouth.

"Why do you care so much?" he said looking for the answer in her eyes.

"Cause it's my job," she said smiling.

"No, it's much more than that. Being a teacher doesn't mean you care. Maybe a little, but not the way you do."

"Well, what can I say? That's just who I am," she said trying not to make a big deal of it.

"So, why me then? Why are you so determined to help me? There must be other students who could use your help."

"Yes, but you need it the most," she said smiling back as she exited the class.

As the day passed on Ellie learned of a Hall Assembly taking place in the afternoon. All classes would be canceled. She was told it was for the Form 5 singing competition, and she could stay in the office and catch up on her marking. There was no need for her to attend, as it was only mandatory for the class teachers. She commented that she would love to join and support her students, but the other teachers snickered at her enthusiasm and returned to chatting amongst themselves.

"Why would you want to go? I wish I wasn't a class teacher; it's such a waste of time," one teacher snarked.

She had wished someone would have told her about such an event in advance, but this was the style of the school and as Ellie would learn, everything happened last minute with little to no warning. You had to be quick to adapt. Or at least check your email every five minutes in hopes of getting an update.

Making her way up to the hall, she noticed a few Form 5 girls nervously prancing about. "I told you, you have to come in with your dance move at the right time!"

"I did, didn't I?"

"Ugh, we wouldn't be having this conversation if you did, Susan!"

Bumping into Ellie, the girl who was being criticized apologized and made her way into the toilet to wipe her eyes. As Ellie entered the hall, students glanced back, whispering amongst themselves. She gave them a thumbs up, trying to show her support. "Good luck guys!" she shouted out, taking a seat in the empty front row, while the lower form students sat chatting amongst themselves behind her. The other teachers were cluttered in the back gossiping about how long this was going to go on and how they had better things to do than watch students try to sing. What a pity, she thought that all these students could clearly feel the resentment of their teachers for simply trying to do a school activity.

As the lights started to fade, feedback from a mic grabbed everyone's attention. "Good to have you all here! I'm Sandy,"

"And I'm Candy!"

"Today, we have 5 classes who will be competing for the title of Singing Champion! So, let's welcome our first class, 5A, who will be singing 'My Heart Will Go On' by Celine Dion."

The crowd erupted, throwing their hands together in a clumsy, off-beat clap. When it finally reached the 5E class's turn to perform, most students' enthusiasm had dimmed. 5E chose to perform 'Hard Feelings' by Lorde and the moment they started, shivers ran up Ellie's spine. Turning to look back at the other teachers, they were still lost in their own little world. She went to turn back around when she noticed Loris' expression sitting horizontally to her a few rows away. His eyes were glazed over as if he was focusing on every lyric that was sung. Staring for a little too long, she caught his attention. He turned to look at her, as she immediately turned back forwards. The lyrics about outgrowing a lover and everyone knowing except for you kept ringing in her ears for the remainder of the day. She knew what it meant and what she was feeling but she still wasn't ready to face it.

Ellie had been married for over twelve years, eloping when she was barely legal. Her husband, twenty-eight at the time, had gotten her pregnant thought the only reasonable thing to do was get married. He possessed the values of a traditional gentleman with the temper of a spoiled child. Unfortunately, at six months, she had a miscarriage and she could tell that her husband blamed her, although he never said it. Childless and married, the high of the honeymoon quickly faded and once-engaging dinnertime conversations became competitions to fill the dead air. Eventually, her husband began traveling for work more frequently. She couldn't remember the last time he had taken her out on a date or complimented her looks. She couldn't even recall the last meal they had together.

"And the winner is… drum roll please! 5E! Congratulations, you guys! You absolutely killed it."

As the whole audience roared in approval, Ellie was brought back to reality. Turning to get up, she noticed Loris was still staring at her, not in a disrespectful way but in curiosity. She was headed back to the staff room when her phone rang.

"Hello?" she answered hesitantly seeing it was her husband.

"I'm flying back out to London tonight. Do you mind picking up my suits later? I'm dropping them off before I head to the airport," he said already expecting her compliance.

"Again? But you just got back last night. I thought it'd be nice if we did something fun this weekend," Ellie said trying to be hopeful, but careful to keep her voice down so students wouldn't overhear her marital drama.

"It's business, Ellie, I'll be back next week." He hung up before Ellie could protest.

Ellie stared at her phone as it returned to the lock screen—one of the first photos they had taken together when she was still young. When she was so sure that she could have a happy ending. Scrolling through her phone, she quickly replaced it with the first photo in her picture scroll. A cute cartoon drawing of her favorite Pokémon: Ninetails.

She knew her husband was a businessman, but she also was smart enough to know that his job did not require the amount of travel he did. When she asked him why he didn't call her when he was away, he would reply that the time zones were too confusing, and he didn't want to disturb her. He claimed he knew she was exhausted from work. A lie she was all too comfortable with. She wondered who was keeping his bed warm at night. Was it one special girl he had grown to love or was he visiting a new one every night satisfying his specific appetite? No matter. Since starting her new job at this school, she had been growing more confident and aware of her self-worth. She had the power to change her situation but still lacked the courage. She just needed a push.

Sinking into her sweats, Netflix and chilling had become her Friday night routine. Her best friend, Clara, called less and less. Her phone screen stared back at her like a black mirror for most, if not all, of the weekend. Her phone would sometimes slip between the couch cushions and remain there till Sunday night. She couldn't be bothered and often forgot about it.

Rummaging through her fridge, she realized she forgot to go grocery shopping. She had forgotten to do a lot of things. Ugh. 11pm. The stores were open 24/7, but that wasn't the issue. The issue was getting the motivation to leave the house when she had already gotten so comfortable. When she had already finished off her first bottle of wine. Fuck it, she thought. I don't need to eat. It's already too late. She grabbed another bottle of wine and walked past the hallway mirror, stopped, and took a look at herself. What would her husband think if he saw her like this? What would her students think knowing the image staring back at her was supposed to be their role model? She shook her head, brushing it off. *Fuck him*, she thought. *I'm going to leave him, even if it takes me a little longer than most people.*

Her eyes suddenly darted towards his office door. She stopped. Her husband had always kept his office door locked, making it clear that he didn't trust his wife with whatever secrets were inside. Ellie lazily turned the knob, not expecting it to give, but to her surprise, it opened without any resistance. The door opened to a sterile, clean office space. Usually in a home office, there would be family photos and other warm reminders. However, file cabinets were the only objects that decorated this office.

Her eyes immediately turned to the computer monitor. She took a seat, spilling a bit of her wine onto the eggshell-colored carpet. Snickering, she tried rubbing it out with her foot but ended up making the stain even worse. She couldn't move the furniture around, or he would know she was snooping around. She decided to let it be tomorrow's problem. Turning on the computer, she waited patiently for the screen to load. When the computer asked her for the login details, she briefly panicked, thinking her husband had chosen something too personal for her to guess. He had become a stranger to her. But after taking another sip, she remembered how simple-minded he could be. Typing in her first guess, his birthday, she was in.

Dozens of zipped folders littered the background, but her attention had been drawn to the background photo—a younger, more beautiful woman lying in a flowerbed of sunflowers laughing. Was this who her husband had been flying to London for? She moved the mouse slowly over each folder, highlighting each one.

"Delete."

"Are you sure you want to move these folders to the recycle bin?"

"Yes."

"Are you sure you want to empty your recycling bin?"

Without hesitation, she confirmed, deleting her husband's entire file collection. She had no idea what had been in those zipped files, but she figured it was a mixture of important work-related documents and inappropriate photos of his extramarital love affair. She couldn't have cared less. She raised her glass to the screen and muttered something she had so long wished she could have said to her husband. "Never again," she said taking one big chug and texting her husband. "Can't wait till you're back. There's a surprise waiting for you," she texted laughing to herself.

An immediate response, "a sexy surprise?" followed by a winky face.

After reading the message and chuckling, she threw her phone out of arm's length not bothering to reply. Eagerly awaiting the bastard's return to see his reaction to what she had just done and how he would take the news of her leaving him, she finished off the second bottle of wine. She had gotten the liquid courage to finally leave him, but it seemed a shame it had taken two whole bottles of wine for her to take a stand.

DAY ONE

CHAPTER 7

Rolling into work on Monday morning, Ellie wore sunglasses that covered up most of her face, even though it was raining heavily, as she could not get motivated to do her makeup beforehand. The sky was pitch black and the rain fell like someone was having a nervous breakdown from heaven. She was feeling like rubbish due to her extra-curricular weekend activities but would pretend to have been up late marking papers. The day passed by as expected. Keeping order in her class was a challenge as students saw a teacher's sickness as an invitation to go crazy in the lessons. Ellie tried her best to keep her classes focused, but her personal life seeped in and mixed with her profession. She had always criticized teachers who were not able to separate the two, stating that what happens at home, stays at home; here she was doing just the opposite. Taking a sip of her coffee, a student approached,

"Miss, can I find you after school?" a hovering Form 6 boy chirped.

"Sure, is there something specific you need help with Thomas?" she asked.

"I just wanted advice about university," he said meeting her eyes.

"Okay, just find me in the staffroom when you're ready," she said rubbing her temple. Today after all, wasn't going to be the interactive-free day she had hoped it would be.

She went for a refill before the first bell rang. Sitting down at her desk, she put her head on the table and closed her eyes. "Deep breaths," she told herself.

"Rough night love?" a colleague asked, getting too close for comfort. It was the P.E. teacher who had given her a hard time about caring about her students before. Why was he invading her personal bubble?

"Something like that."

"You really shouldn't be out so late, especially on a school night, love," he said, jumping to assumptions.

"Are you kidding me?" She was sick of being condescended to. "I'm sick."

"Whatever you say, love. You know it's interesting, though, how you spend so much of your time with students after hours. Maybe that's why you're so tired, huh?"

"What does that mean?" She grew defensive.

"I'm just saying, you don't see many teachers having dim sum with their students at midnight, especially when they have school the next day."

It was a weird thing to bring up when it had happened months ago. "You were watching me?"

"Passing by is all and just happened to see you two. I think Mrs. Green would be interested to know how you spend your free time."

Ellie immediately thought the worst. If he had seen them there, had he followed them to the park? Did he see Loris try to kiss her? No, there was no way. She hadn't done anything wrong and wouldn't be made to feel that way.

"I don't appreciate your insinuations," she challenged.

"Hmm..." he smirked, looking her up and down. "Nothing to get angry about, love. It's just interesting is all. And, it happened to be Loris of all students. How interesting."

"I don't need to explain myself to you."

"You're right, but you might have to explain yourself to Mrs. Green," he said pleased with himself.

She was in no mood to deal with his shit or any other outspoken colleagues. She grabbed her coffee and stormed out to the roof-top to sneak a cigarette. She wasn't a regular smoker but, since starting at this school, she had picked up the habit. She lit up the strawberry-flavored cigarette she had gotten as a souvenir from her friend when visiting Japan and leaned out over the railing. No one ever came up here besides the janitors every few months or so. Tarps and plastic sheets filled the floor of the roof from renovations they had started until the money ran out. She doubted it would ever be finished.

"Fancy seeing you here," Loris startled her, causing her to throw the cigarette over the railing to avoid being caught... *Shit. If someone finds that, it's going to raise a lot of questions. Where did it even land?*

"What are you doing here, Loris? You shouldn't be up here."

"Neither should you, Miss," he offered her another cigarette.

She rejected it. "I'm ok."

"But you had no problem smoking until I showed up."

"Yeah, that's right."

"Huh..." He put the pack away.

"You know, someone saw us that night."

"What do you mean?"

"I mean, when we went out to dim sum, when we talked."

"So? We weren't doing anything wrong? You were helping me, or at least trying to convince me to let you."

"I know that, but it could have looked..."

"Nonsense. Who saw us?"

"One of the teachers here."

"So, what? What are they going to do?"

"He said he might go to Mrs. Green."

"And say what? It's not illegal to have dinner with your teacher."

"It's not that simple."

"Are you ok? You must be feeling pretty shit about it."

"Yeah, I'll be ok. Just please, Loris, it's less than two months to graduation. Let's get you there, ok? Then you don't have to deal with this bullshit again."

"How about you though? Are you still planning on working here?"

"It's my job; I can't exactly leave."

He sighed and his eyes grew soft. Their situations were a bit different. "Just don't know why everyone is giving you such a hard time. They're just jealous."

"Maybe."

"Anyways, don't worry. I'm not going to let you down. I got this," he said, trying to get her to smile.

It worked, even if just for a moment. "Ok, I trust you."

He left down the stairs, leaving her alone. He always seemed to be coming and going, popping out when she least expected it. He was everywhere. She didn't see him for the rest of the day... she wasn't sure if that was a good or bad thing.

After school, the Form 6 boy, Thomas, as promised, approached, "May I speak to Ellie, please?" a voice echoed from the intercom into the staffroom, alerting every teacher nearby.

"Wow, you sure are popular!" "So busy, Ellie!" the teachers commented. If only it wasn't so repetitive all the time; it was getting old. And she couldn't keep laughing it off for much longer. It was only a matter of time until she snapped.

Walking out and motioning him to the table outside where students usually sat with their teachers to get homework help, she sat down next to him and welcomed him to begin. "So, what's up?" she said focusing all of her attention onto him.

"Well, we only have three weeks left of school before we start self-studying at home for the DSE. Everyone else seems to have a plan or at least an idea of what they want to do after finishing secondary school, but I still have no clue," he said discouraged.

"Don't worry, you're not the only one. When I was your age, I also had no idea what I wanted to do. I felt like I had two options: join the military or start working immediately. What do you like doing?" she said trying to lift his spirits. But as he started speaking, vibrations coming from Ellie's phone interrupted them. She turned her phone over, trying hard to ignore it. But every time the ringing died down, it started again.

"Sorry, let me just see who's calling, and I'll be right back," she said knowing very well it was her husband. *Why was he calling? He never called.* Excusing herself to the elevator corridor, she hesitantly answered, the courage she had built up from the weekend before, was quickly dwindling.

Answering the phone, she remained silent. "You bitch, do you know what you've done!" an angry voice shouted. Anyone within five feet would have been able to hear him.

"Excuse me? Don't talk to me that way," she said.

"Excuse me? That's all you have to say for yourself?" he continued.

She realized that her husband was no longer in London and put two and two together. *Shit. Why was he home already when he told her he'd be gone till next week?*

"What are you talking about?" she asked, pretending she had no idea what he was going on about.

"You fucking bitch! Don't pretend you don't know what you did. Deleting all of my files for work, my company is going to kill me. I could lose my job," he said with an escalating voice.

She couldn't care less. "Maybe you should have treated me better then. You brought this on yourself," she said with no emotion.

"When you get home, I swear to god..."

"What, are you going to hit me again?" she said sarcastically, cupping her hand over her mouth so no one could hear. She was full of rage.

"You know full well what I'll do," he said now screaming at the top of his lungs.

The phone was practically vibrating out of her hand from the noise. Growing frustrated and trying to keep her cool as she was still in the role of teacher, she remained calm, trying to think of what to say. But as her silence filled the air, she felt as if she could feel the screaming of her husband surround her, echoing and filling the school corridor. It felt as if the screams had a closer connection to her than just over the speaker of her phone. She couldn't deal with it.

She hung up while he was still yelling and walked back towards the patiently waiting student as if nothing had happened. But her insides were still shaking. As she approached, she could still hear her husband's screams reverberating around her, it had penetrated her mind. Trying to ignore it, she sat down.

"Sorry about that. Now, you were saying?"

But the boy was distracted and did not notice his teacher's return. Trying to regain his attention, she placed her hand on his shoulder, "What is it?" she asked confused as she began to notice the horror reflecting from his eyes. The screams, she realized, were not those of her husband's, but of students and staff close by. They grew louder, coming from below as every second passed. Confused, she watched the student stand up and walk towards the staircase carefully to see what was going on.

"Hey, wait a second!" she called out, but the student didn't hear her. He made his way down the staircase, sprinting towards the sound. Ellie tried to follow after him, but it was too late. As she made her way to the top of the staircase, she saw the boy get grabbed and dragged down the remaining flight of stairs. Frozen in horror, she watched two agile figures rip him away from the railing. Screaming for his life, one of the creatures swiftly bit into his jugular as the other tore into his abdomen, tearing with its razor-sharp teeth that looked like they were slivered shards of pointed glass. Blood spat out like a water fountain on its last legs. His eyes turned to her as he let out his last breath. He looked so scared; he knew he was going to die. Ellie couldn't look away.

Their grotesque bodies were made for killing. They weren't just killing for sport but they were devouring the flesh of their prey. Their bodies had a dark complexion and they were tall and slender with loose skin hanging from their arms and abdomen area. Their bodies had an unusual skeletal structure that Ellie had not seen before. It looked stable yet flexible, allowing it to bend into unnatural and impossible positions. Their faces were pointed and their mouths took up half of their faces. The lines of their mouths looked like they had been sliced to give them more space. They had bulging black veins and protruding red eyes. They were ravenous. They seemed to rely on their other senses more so than their sight but they could still see. Ellie also noticed they had no visible nose. They looked like they had popped right out of a scene from one of her favorite horror movies. She was waiting for someone to yell 'cut' like all of this was for shooting a movie scene.

Ellie screamed, immediately covering her mouth while she slowly backed away from the brutal scene. There was nothing she could do. It was too late for him. Looking around the corridor, it was still empty. Whatever had grabbed the student didn't seem to have made its way up to the second floor where she was yet. She immediately went into survival mode and rushed around, trying to find a way to escape. She moved from classroom to classroom peering into the windows, checking for students. Empty. No signs of life. She then remembered that there had been an outing for all S2 students earlier in the day, so it made sense that all the classrooms were empty. Rushing into the staffroom, she tried to open the door, but it was locked shut. She had left her staff card at her desk and had no way of getting inside without it. Technology had screwed her again.

Trying not to bring attention to herself, she knocked quietly, but fiercely.

"Is anyone inside? Please let me in, something is happening in the school!" Hearing the door unlock, the gym teacher quickly pulled her inside, locking the door behind her and grasped her arms. She could see the fear in his eyes.

"What's going on?" Ellie demanded, shaking him off. She could see the look of fear in his eyes.

"No one knows. We're lucky to have made it here," he said panting.

"We have to get everyone out of the school immediately, especially the students!" she said pacing back and forth. "I just saw one boy get dragged away and something was eating him alive," Ellie said, realizing how crazy she sounded.

"We need to stay here!" he protested. "Whatever is out there is out for blood. We can't handle it on our own. We are only teachers! It's too late for them, but we can still save ourselves" he said clearly unwilling to risk his own survival to save students.

"But we have to make sure all the students are safe or at least try to save the ones who are left. I think whatever it is hasn't made its way up to the 2/F yet, so that means all the students on the above floors still have time!" she said pleading, hoping to change his mind.

Turning away from her, he coldly said, "You're on your own. I have my family to think about. You should do the same. If you decide to go back out there, this door will be locked, and I will not open it again."

What family? He lived with a roommate and his cat that he never shut up about.

Unable to accept his harsh words, she ran to her desk, grabbed her backpack and threw everything she could fit inside, including her makeup and a plethora of snacks. Old habits die hard. Rushing out of the door, she looked back at her colleague, "You know, people like you deserve to die," she kicked the door so hard that it bent at the hinges, unable to be properly locked again. As she ran up to the third floor, as he shouted out profanities behind her. No one would save him now. She took a certain comfort in knowing that.

Making her way through the third and fourth floor, she could not find any students. It was after school. *Maybe they've all gone home.* But she couldn't give up yet; she had to make sure there was no one left. After making her way to the last room, the multipurpose room, she saw the light on. Slowly opening the door, she went inside, cautiously checking for any students. No one. Satisfied that she had done her job, she went to leave when she saw what she thought to be two students walking in her direction.
"Are you guys ok?" she yelled out, being careful not to be too loud.

She started rushing towards them, but she soon wished she hadn't. As she approached, she noticed their blood-stained mouths and sharp teeth. Strips of shredded flesh hung from one of their mouths, impaled on one of the teeth. Ellie started to retreat backwards never taking her eyes off of them. The tallest one screeched out, sprinting towards her as the other followed closely behind. Ellie turned and rushed back into the multipurpose room, switched off the lights, and ducked behind a row of foldable chairs farthest away from the door. Cupping her hands over her mouth to silence her breathing, she heard the door swing open forcefully, followed by a loud crash that shattered one of the mirrors covering the adjacent wall.

It echoed all around her. She could not center herself; she had lost focus and began sweating nervously. As the two figures grew closer to her, they destroyed everything in their path. With one swipe of their claw-like hands, the foldable chairs went flying to the side of the room. The figures walked over the shards of glass that now covered the wooden floor. They were so focused on finding her. She watched their paw-like feet with 2-inch sharp curved nails step onto the jagged edges without effect. The glass crunched under their feet, leaving no trace of blood. One of the creatures flung the teacher's podium across the room. It splintered from the impact and laid spewed out across the floor; nothing more than debris. Soon there would be nothing left standing between them and her. Looking around, she realized the mirrors gave her away, not just reflecting light from the windows but revealing her location as well. The creatures hadn't seemed to notice yet, but it was only a matter of time. Her breath grew louder, despite her best efforts to muffle it out. Her nervous asthma certainly wasn't helping any.

Closing her eyes, she tried to re-center herself and imagine that she was somewhere else, somewhere where her skin would soak up the sun. This dream was soon interrupted by a deafening screech that sounded like a dying animal from the tallest monster. He finally discovered her reflection in the mirror and charged straight at the wall, teeth chattering, closely followed by the second. As the glass from all the mirrors shattered, she knew this was her opportunity to get out. Without looking back, she darted towards the only other exit. She put all her weight into the door, but it didn't budge. The door was jammed. Frozen in fear, she feared this was it. She didn't have to turn around to see the two figures making their way towards her and know that she would end up just like the Form 6 boy. She squeezed her eyes shut and braced for the worst when suddenly the door crashed open. Before she could comprehend what was happening, she was dragged out and ordered to run!

"Don't look back," the voice shouted.

It was Loris.

CHAPTER 8

Every second was precious now. Going down was not an option; the only way out was up. As they ascended to the top floor as fast as they could, they reached the gate to the rooftop. It was bolted. Of all the times for the janitors to come up and lock the gate... The only way to get past was to climb over, and in the hysteric state Ellie was in, that would prove to be a challenge.

"Here, grab my hand," Loris said, reaching down to help her get over the spiked gate.

She turned to look back, but Loris quickly drew her attention back to the escape plan.

"Don't look back. We don't have time. Quickly, give me your hand," he said in frustration. Given the circumstances, he was strangely calm.

Ellie grabbed his hand, propped herself up, and slid her legs over the gate. She jumped down, landing in Loris' arms. Both his hands were now on her waist for support. But she was too shaken up to pull away.

"We need to keep going," he said leading her away from the gate in a crouched position, trying not to draw any more attention to themselves. As they reached the ledge of the school that joined the two buildings, they overlooked a horizon of mangled bodies spread across the schoolyard. The mysterious monsters--ravenous, all moving in a predatory fashion, circled the ones who had tried to escape. Some people were still fighting for their lives, but their screams and the crack of breaking bones snapping gave no hope. The sounds of flesh ripping apart rang louder than the school bell had ever done in both their ears. There was no hope for those left behind.

Retreating, they moved away from the gate and took shelter inside the maintenance shed on the rooftop, hoping to wait it out while simultaneously wishing this was all just a bad dream and they had both been in each other's nightmares. But they both knew this was something they might never wake up from.

"Here," Loris said, handing Ellie a warped, slightly dirty tarp that looked like it had been used to cover plants. He unraveled it and spread it across her like a blanket. It crunched slightly as he wrapped it around her. She retreated into it, curling her legs up into her chest still trying to convince herself this wasn't real. Loris searched around the shed for other supplies that they might be able to use but came back with only a pack of water bottles, gardener gloves, duct tape, a duffle bag, and a straw hat. He loaded everything into the duffle bag, all except for the straw hat for obvious reasons. There was no way he could see either of them using it, so he tossed it aside. He feared it was probably the nesting ground for spiders laying their eggs. There was nothing more he was afraid of than spiders, a secret he had managed to keep and planned on keeping.

"What.....were those things...?" Ellie said looking up for the first time since everything had happened.

"I have no idea," Loris said sitting down next to her, moving closer.

"I saw one.... rip apart a student like it was nothing. I had just been talking to him and then suddenly he was gone. Just like that. I tried to stop him. I knew something was off, but he just kept going. He didn't even look back. The look on his face when they got him was....It was just so.....surprised..."

"I know," Loris said comforting her. "I was upstairs smoking when it all happened and when I saw..."

"Wait, how did you know where I was," she suddenly interrupted, turning to him.

"I saw you run into the room and those two....things, whatever the hell they were, followed you inside."

"But why would you go back down when you saw those things?" she said now staring directly at him, pure confusion in her eyes.

"You're seriously asking me why I saved your life instead of saying thank you right now?" he said in disbelief, shaking his head. "You're unbelievable."

"No...I, of course I'm grateful.....I just don't understand why. You could have been killed."

"I wasn't thinking about that. I just knew I had to do something and make sure you were safe," he said with no hesitation.

"I should be the one saving you, saving all those other students out there," she said trying to get up, but tears starting to flow from her eyes and she became weak thinking about all the other students whom she had let down. If she hadn't been so preoccupied with talking to her husband, she would have at least been able to save that boy, she thought.

"Stop," he said as he pulled her back down. She leaned against the wall as the gravity of what had just happened hit her hard. Loris grabbed her hand and guided her towards the bed he had made out of the tarp and a pillow using his own hoodie.

It wasn't much but it would have to do.

"It's going to be okay," he said as he tucked her in. He would stand guard for the night.

"Don't worry," he said. "I won't let anything happen to you."

But Ellie was all too familiar with making promises that were beyond one's control. She wouldn't be able to sleep knowing that those things were still out there. Every time she tried to close her eyes, the brutality she witnessed earlier kept playing in a loop. She couldn't escape it. She kept her eyes open and became fixated on the unintentional patterns on the walls.

CHAPTER 9

Her eyes went into autopilot mode and she didn't realize how much time had passed. It felt like hours but it could have just been minutes. She was so disoriented and in shock. After what had felt like forever, it appeared to be the middle of the night. Loris was gazing out the door when she startled him by talking.

"Shit, you scared me," he said turning around abruptly.

"What time is it?" she said rubbing her eyes. "And where am I?"

"No clue, my phone's dead, and I don't have a watch," he said, turning back to the door.

Checking her phone, she saw it was 4am. She had 50 missed calls and over 40 new voicemails. Her battery was at 10%. Why hadn't she put her phone on battery saving mode? Or the better question she was beating herself up over was why hadn't she immediately called to check on all of the people close to her to make sure they were ok? Most of the calls she assumed would be from her husband, and she couldn't care less about him. But she was worried about Clara. Had whatever happened here happened everywhere else too? What did it mean? She dialed her best friend's number hoping to hear she was wrong, but it went straight to voicemail. She went to check her voicemail immediately, assuming the worst.

5:55pm: "Ellie, where are you? They're telling us we need to evacuate now, and I can't reach Tom." Tom was her husband. "Do you know what's happening?! I've tried calling, but I can't get through. Your husband has been calling me too. Please let me know that you're ok."

6:30pm: "Still no word from Tom. I've packed what I can. They told us to just bring a bag, nothing more, and meet at one of the evacuation points in Central or Chai Wan. The Chinese border has shut down and isn't letting anyone in. I'm scared Ellie. I can't leave without him."

7:35pm: "Ellie! Where are you? Why aren't you answering your phone! I need you. I fucking need you to answer your phone and tell me you're ok! I'm with Tom and your husband right now waiting at the evacuation point in Chai Wan, and their loading up the ships. They're going to close the gates soon. You need to get here, NOW! Please hurry. They're telling people who can't make it to get to one of the typhoon shelters for safety. Please be safe."

8:00: "Ellie, please, I need you to listen to me, I don't know if I'm going to get another chance to say it, but I love you. I need you to know that. They've stopped letting people in here, it's too late. Don't come to..." the message cut off abruptly.

End of new messages.

"Fuck," she said hitting her hand against the wall. "Fuck, fuck, fuck, fuck, fuck." Maybe they had gotten on the boat and she lost service or her cellphone died. That had to have been it. She couldn't face the possibility that her best friend was gone. But why did the last message suddenly cut off? Was she saying that they stopped letting people in after she had gotten on the boat? What did it mean?

"Shhh, calm down. They might still be out there," Loris said grabbing her hands and stroking them. It seemed to be working.

"I... I don't understand...she just..." she said spiraling further into her panic attack.

"Here just lay down," he said motioning towards the bed. "There's nothing we can do right now."

"But what about the monsters," she said still clutching her phone for dear life, retreating into the mentality of a child's.

"I'll protect you," he said gently like a father would to his daughter. He tucked her back in, hiding the truth in his eyes. He had to be strong for both of them. The roles had suddenly shifted. Ellie fought as hard as she could to stay awake but she was exhausted.

DAY 2

As the sun rose the next day, rays of light snuck into the cracks of the shed, bouncing off and getting caught in the glass jars, illuminating the room with a feeling of hope. But the usual sounds of nature welcoming a new day were absent, leaving behind loud and echoing. Loris had fallen asleep sitting next to Ellie holding a knife in his. "WAKE UP! WAKE UP!" Her phone alarm started playing the most obnoxious wail. Ellie had picked it long ago to ensure she would actually get up for work on time during the week. And what a way to start your morning with a reminder of how suddenly things had changed. Jolting up and hitting her head on the wall in a sudden rush, she scrambled to turn her alarm off. Her eyes were still blurry and crusty from sleeping and she struggled to find the right buttons. Loris grabbed her phone and turned it off immediately.

"Seriously," he said using his fingers to massage his temple. He got up and peeked out to make sure the loud alarm hadn't given away their position to the creatures. The coast was clear for now. "Of all things, this happens. It's better it's off anyways, save your battery," he said giving her back the phone.

"Hey, thanks for taking care of me last night and for everything, I was a mess," she said with genuine thanks, regaining her composure.

"Of course, I wasn't about to leave you," he said.

She felt like she had become a burden to him. Would he still be trapped on this rooftop if he hadn't saved her? During all of the chaos, she was still over-thinking unnecessary things.

"Did you look outside yet?" she said getting up.

"Not yet."

"It's weird, you know. Having it be morning and the sun is shining, but I can't hear any birds. There's absolutely no sound. I mean, where are they?" she said confused.

They eased out of the shed and crept out to the roof's edge, knowing what they would see. Bodies. Lots of bodies. But the streets and school yard were clear. Nothing was there. Just blood. Lots of dried up blood where the bodies had been the night before.

"What the fuck? Where the fuck did they go?" Ellie said frantically, searching around.

Loris ran to the other side of the ledge and was met with the same scene. Lots of blood and personal items skewed across the yard but no bodies.

"This is....fucked up."

"No kidding," Ellie said, sarcastically. "I mean, we saw them die. There was no way they were getting out of that. Did those things eat them all, their whole bodies?" not believing herself as she said it.

"Those things...I think they might be zombies," Loris said without hesitation.

"Like in the movies?! They can't be real!"

"Then how do you explain what happened?"

"I don't know, but that's crazy."

"I know it sounds crazy but it's the only thing that makes sense right now. All those people down there were bitten!"

"So, you're saying that they're zombies now too, and that's why there are no bodies? They just got up and walked away?!"

Loris scrunched his face up and kept changing his expression. He opened his mouth a few times like he was about to speak but kept hesitating.

"We need to get out of here," Loris said heading back into the shed to grab his stuff. They couldn't stay here. He threw everything into his bag and checked the shed one last time for any supplies he might have missed.

"And go where?" Ellie asked, although she knew her question was pointless.

"Let's go back down and check the school for supplies first, and then we'll figure it out."

As they walked back down to the gate, they noticed all the classrooms were dark--the power had gone out. It figured. This was going to make things more difficult. Loris went first, cautiously checking ahead to make sure there weren't any surprises waiting for them.

"All clear!" he said motioning for her to join him. They walked together, Loris always a few steps ahead, checking the classrooms for anything of value they might be able to take with them. After searching each floor, they managed to find a few half empty bottles of water, candy, and a few exacto knives. Why students always had exacto knives in their stationary boxes was still a mystery to Ellie. But, in this situation, she wasn't complaining. Ellie grabbed a box of number 9 pens and a blank notebook from a teacher's desk, placing it carefully into her bag. It seemed so important to her at that moment to have a way to write. Before they left, they reached the staff room. Ellie stood in front of the staffroom door she had broken that was now sprayed with blood. Only now could she fully realize the horrendous consequences of her actions of breaking the latch on the door when she left. When that teacher told her it'd be locked and he wouldn't open it again. She was so angry that she said he deserved to die. She meant it at the time but seeing the door made her question herself. She couldn't downplay what was right in front of her like she normally could. It was a talent really. Every time she would find herself in a less than ideal situation regarding her husband and her life, she managed to contort and twist reality into a comfortable lie.

"Ellie, are you ok?" Loris said noticing the look of horror on her face.

"It's nothing, let's check here before we leave," she said pushing past the door, walking straight towards her desk. She kept her eyes forward and didn't let herself steal any side glances in fear for what she might see.

"We need to be quick," Loris said, keeping a lookout. "We don't know how long we'll be safe here."

Ellie finished gathering her stuff and threw on the jacket she had left at her desk. She went to leave when she saw the picture frame on her desk of her husband and her. They looked happy there. Could have fooled anyone. It fooled her. She picked it up and threw it onto the ground, glass shards smashing everywhere.

Loris, standing right beside her, dared not to interfere.

"Ready?" he asked.

"Yeah, luckily I have a blanket and a mini pantry at my desk with power bars and other snacks," she said half-smiling, hoping it would be enough.

"Why do you have a blanket? Not that I'm complaining. Just seems so random," Loris raised his brow. "It gets cold in here. Even in winter, they crank up the air conditioner and refuse to let any of us turn it off."
"Damn, that sucks."

"So, where are we going?" she asked intently.

"We need to go somewhere familiar and close. My dad's home is just a few minutes' walk away. Let's go there first," he said throwing his backpack over his shoulder.

As they were leaving, Ellie suddenly remembered the emergency kit that was kept under the sink. She hurried over and grabbed it, quickly checking the contents. Basic first aid supplies and two flashlights with extra batteries. She chucked it in her bag and followed behind Loris.

CHAPTER 10

Still looking for answers, they walked down the streets carefully, sticking to the alleys and avoiding the main roads. It was still quiet, too quiet. There were no people around and this was a city of 7 million. Abandoned cars littered the streets, doors left open and keys still in the ignition. Bicycles lay turned over on the sidewalks along with shopping bags.

"This is just too weird," Ellie said. "If what attacked us were zombies, they would be everywhere."

"I mean that's just from the movies though, there's no way to tell truth from fiction right now. All we know is that whatever these things are, they bite people and feast on them. Then those people disappear," Loris said picking up his pace. "We're almost there."

They got to the front of an apartment complex and Loris tugged the gate open. The lock pad had been deactivated when the power went out. Reaching the 17th floor wasn't easy by foot but on the bright side, it seemed like none of the monsters had gotten inside yet. As they reached Loris' door, another door creaked open down the hall. A frail elderly couple stood there looking out at them curiously.

"Excuse me?" Ellie said taking a step towards them. The couple retreated before she could approach them, dead bolting what sounded like five locks that were behind the door. *What had they seen?*

"Ignore them, they won't be any help to us. They're both senile" he said opening his apartment door.

Ellie had never been to one of her students' homes before. She had always imagined getting an invite from a parent who wanted to show their appreciation for all of her effort, but that day never came. It wasn't how she imagined Loris' home to be. She hadn't spent much time imagining it before, but it certainly wasn't like this.

"Just wait right here for a sec," he said checking the room furthest away. The coast was clear.

"We should be fine here for a while," he said locking the main door and throwing his stuff down. Ellie sat on the worn-out red leather sofa and grabbed a throw pillow, hugging it tightly. Loris came back a few minutes later with a small rectangular cardboard box. Inside was an old-school broadcasting radio. He turned it on and scanned the channels for something familiar. Static swept across the lanes until he finally landed on a signal.

"This is an emergency broadcast. All residents should remain inside until further notice. I repeat—do not go outside under any circumstances until further notice. We are doing everything we can to ensure your safety. Safety measures have been put in place. Code: 15977520.

The message repeated over and over again but no matter how many times they heard it, it still didn't make sense.

"That code...what does it mean?"

He put down the radio and hung his head in his hands. "I want to give you answers but I don't have them." He avoided eye contact when he said it.

"Sorry I was talking out loud, I didn't mean to put this on you," she said seeing his body tense up.

"Are you thirsty?" he said changing the subject.

"Water's fine," she replied.

"Water? Are you sure? After all this shit has just happened, you don't want anything stronger?" he said pouring himself a glass of whisky. It was clear he had done this before. Ellie didn't want to be a bad influence, but then realized how stupid that sounded. She had just seen people literally get eaten and here she was worried about accepting alcohol from a minor.

"You know what, make it a double... no, a triple," she said suddenly realizing how badly she needed a drink.

Handing her the glass, they clinked glassed together without words. It had already been a long day even though it was just beginning.

"We can stay here until we figure out what's going on. Sorry it's not cleaner," he said apologizing.

"I didn't even notice," she said finishing her drink. Her mind was still preoccupied with the horrifying messages she received. Were Clara and her husband both ok? Or were they dead? Did she even really care? She didn't know anymore. Placing the glass down on the table, she noticed a card with a cartoon dog blowing out candles--a birthday card. Curious, she opened it and saw it was addressed to Loris.

"Wish I could be there to celebrate with you!" it read.

"From my mum. She took off when I was four," he said pouring himself another glass. "This is just her way of trying to make herself feel better for abandoning me." He filled hers up generously without asking.

"I'm sorry," she said uncomfortably, crossing her legs.

"Why?" he asked confused.

"It just sounds complicated," she said trying not to overstep her boundaries.

"Yeah, story of my life. How about your family? Is it also complicated?"

"You could say that."

"Where are they now?"

"I wouldn't know, I haven't talked to them in over 11 years. But I guess they're still in the same place as before."

Loris took a long sip and swirled the remaining whisky around the bottom of the glass.

"So, when is your birthday?" Ellie asked to change the subject. She didn't want to talk about her estranged family. There was too much bad blood and not enough time to get into it. She didn't want to waste the time they had on that now.

"Yesterday," he said throwing the card in the bin. It had hit a nerve.

Yesterday--when all of that shit was going down, it was his birthday. And she thought she had the worst luck when it came to the big day. After 29 birthdays, she still hadn't been captured on film smiling for any of them—for reasons still unknown. Maybe it was the disappointment of it all. One day being hyped up and the reality of the actual day not quite living up to your expectations.

"Pretty crap way to celebrate, huh?" he said trying to lighten the mood.

"Yeah," she laughed but it sounded forced.

"Well, good news is, I'm legal now, Miss," he said winking. Alcohol had almost brought him back to his old cheeky self.

"Oh, get out of here!" she said throwing one of the couch pillows at him. He still managed to have his twisted sense of humor. Good for him.

As nightfall approached, they both grew sleepy. Neither of them had slept well the previous night and being able to sleep in a real bed was alluring to them both.

Ellie was comfortably buzzed on the couch while Loris contemplated which room she could sleep in. His dad's was a mess and his was only slightly better.

"You can sleep in my room tonight," he said. "The bed's made, and it'll be more comfortable."

"Where will you sleep, though?"

"In my dad's, no worries. Not expecting him back anytime soon, all things considering."

"Don't say that. Do you want to try and call him? I think my phone has enough power to make a call," she said getting up and walking towards him.

"I'm just being realistic and anyways, it wouldn't be the worst thing. He's a dick. Even if I did try to call him, he wouldn't answer the phone even with all this happening. He blames me for her leaving, you know," referring to his mom.

Ellie could relate a little too well to everything he had said. He led her to his room. His bed was made up with a thick dark blue comforter. The sheets... dark blue as well. He had no curtains on his window and the walls were littered with paintings and drawings.

"Did you do all these?" She stared at the paintings. They were so dark and twisted. She was absolutely fascinated with them.

"Yeah, it helps me think." He went to his closet, took out one of his long t-shirts and gym shorts, and handed them to Ellie.

"You can shower if you'd like. Haven't used the hot water heater since yesterday, so there still should be a whole tank left. There's a towel in the bathroom."

"Thanks," she said grabbing the clothes and shutting the door.

She quickly undressed and started the water. She felt an immediate sense of relief. She always felt safer in the water. It was a familiar comfort. As she washed all the debris off herself, she watched the brown water circle the drain. She got lost in thought and almost felt like everything was normal again. She was almost at the point of convincing herself that this was all a bad dream. Almost. After finishing, she quickly checked to make sure there was still enough hot water left for Loris. She was nothing if not considerate. As she walked out of the room, she saw Loris shirtless looking out of the window.

"Feel better?" he said turning around.

"Much. What are you looking at?" she asked trying not to stare but she couldn't help it. He was too distracted to notice.

"Just thought I heard something outside. It's hard to see with all this fog, but I swear I saw something moving around. They both looked out the window staring intensely. There was nothing.

"There should be some hot water left," she said heading towards the bedroom.

"Thanks," he said. "Sweet dreams."

"You too," she turned and looked back.

As she laid in bed, she stared at the ceiling covered with glowing stick-on stars that reminded her of her childhood. She hadn't seen those since she was a kid. She felt a nostalgic kind of comfort. She imagined the memory of her early mother when she was still a child. She was here telling her that she just had a bad dream and that in the morning everything would be ok.

CHAPTER 11

They had made it half-way through the night when they were awakened by the screams of a neighbor. Ellie, paralyzed with fear, couldn't move from the bed. It wasn't until Loris came and got her that she snapped out of it.

"What is that?" she said shaking. She wanted to curl up and hide under the covers and wait for this nightmare to be over. Loris kneeled next to the bed.

"Shh, keep quiet. It's coming from one of the neighbor's." They both quietly got up and walked towards the main door but every step they made sounded like they were walking on broken glass. Ellie slowly opened the peep hole to look. She covered her mouth and stepped back into Loris' arms to keep from falling over. She covered her mouth and whispered, "They're, they're here."

Loris grabbed her shoulders, looking deep into her eyes. He didn't need to ask who.

"The monsters...they...." she said covering her mouth again. "They got inside."

Loris stepped forward and peered out and saw that a group of them had broken into the flat across the hall. It was Lauren. His childhood friend had spent many nights on the stoop with him when his dad was too drunk and angry for him to come home. He went for the lock on the door when Ellie pulled him back.

"What are you doing? If they know we're here, they'll kill us," she said in disbelief.

He wanted more than anything to help Lauren, but Ellie was right. It was useless. The creatures were already in the flat and, judging by the blood curdling screams, it was already too late. He stepped away from the door and walked behind his couch, slowly pushing it towards the door.

Ellie helped him move it, hoping it would be enough to shield them from the threat. The rest of the night, they stayed together sitting against the wall, staring at the door waiting to see if something tried to get in. They didn't say a word. The screams had finally stopped. They knew they could be next. They had to leave.

DAY 3

In the morning, the sun shined bright. They went to the door and peered out the peephole, but no one was there. Only blood and carnage of the night remained. They smelt something awful so Loris carefully unlocked and opened the door to take a closer look. The smell permeated the whole hallway. He peered out slowly and immediately was drawn to his left. Smoke was seeping out of the bottom crack of the door belonging to the elderly couple they saw last night. Loris ran to the door and tried to open it, but it was still locked. Charcoal. The smell wafted out heavier and they both realized what had happened. "They must have heard what the same thing we did and couldn't bear to live with it, they knew it was only a matter of time," Ellie said walking up behind him.

They both pressed against the door and tried to force it open, but it was bolted from inside.

"At least they went out on their own terms together," he said walking away. They stopped outside of Lauren's door. It was wide open and quiet inside. They didn't need to take a second look to notice the blood caked into the carpet. Almost crusted. Loris took a deep breath and took a step in. Ellie pulled him back.

"She was your friend. Let me go first," she said, stepping in, afraid of what she knew he'd see.

He didn't argue. Loris' shoulders were drooping, and his eyes were blot shot. He didn't have any expression on his face so she couldn't tell what he was feeling except for exhausted. His hair had started matting up and sticking out.

She slowly walked in, her eyes darting back and forth so furiously, it would make anyone dizzy. The trails of blood led to the kitchen and smack-dab in the middle of the floor tiles was a pool of blood that had gravitated toward the center.

"Is she there?" Loris couldn't bear to look.

"No," Ellie said confused. She noticed a bloodied knife next to the puddle. It looked like Lauren had tried to defend herself. She walked through the rest of the flat searching for any clue. She got back to the kitchen to see Loris standing over the puddle, clenching his fists.

"Where is she?" he said just as puzzled.

"I don't know. It's just like school. They...just disappear."

"People don't just disappear. She must have escaped somehow." "She's gone Loris, I'm sorry," Ellie said, placing her hand on his shoulder.

He shook it off. He was looking for someone to blame, and she was the closest person.

"We should get going. We're not safe here anymore," he said heading back.

"And go where?" Ellie questioned.

"I don't know, but we need to leave tonight."

CHAPTER 12

Loris sat on the couch while Ellie gathered her stuff.

"I don't even know what to bring," he said.

"Bring something that reminds you of who you were. And food. We don't know what it's gonna be like out there."

Curious at her response, he stood up. "I don't even know who I am right now."

"I'm still trying to figure that out, too," she said.

Coming out of his room, he had his jacket and cap in one hand and a duffle bag in the other.

"You ready?" she asked.

Loris threw her a jacket and a scarf.

"Here, might get cold."

She smiled, "So, what did you pack?"

He ignored her question and started to head out.

I guess it's personal, she thought.

As they left the flat, Loris took one last look back.

"You know, I spent my whole life in this shithole that was disguised as a home. I know it's probably safer to stay at least until we can figure out what is going on but anywhere is better than here."

"I understand," Ellie said rubbing his shoulder.

"I just think we can do better."

Ellie already had somewhere in mind.

"I'm not gonna miss it one bit." Loris' eyes lit up just a little when he said that.

They headed out right just as dusk pressed back against the light. They figured they'd draw the least attention and be less visible. They hadn't really discussed what the plan was, but Ellie had one place she wanted to go. She needed closure. Her home wasn't too far away. They could make it, she thought. She just didn't know how to tell Loris. She felt awkward bringing him to her home, but it made no sense as she was just at his. She still wasn't ready to fully let go of the formalities.

"Hey, we need to stop somewhere first," she managed to get out.

"Well… it's not like we have anywhere we need to be, so what's one stop."

"I just need to get something from my home," she added.

Loris, curious, turned to her, "so you're taking me home, Miss?" he joked.

Her face turned bright red and she let out an unexpected laugh.

Before she could say anything, he added, "Sorry, couldn't help it."

They had been walking for about twenty minutes, mainly sticking to the alley ways before they first heard it. It was a high pitch scream that echoed in their ears. Ellie froze. The monsters couldn't have been far. And it was only a matter of time until they would reach them. Looking around, they had two options: go onto the main road or try and break into one of the small shops nearby. Loris, without speaking, ran up to one of the 7-11s and tried pulling up the shutter door; it was impossible. All the shutters had been locked with a combination lock All it did was make sound which alerted the monsters to their presence.

"We need to go, now!" Ellie yanked at Loris' sleeve as he went to try another shop.

He kept pulling, trying his luck.

She grabbed his arm, pulled him away and started running. *Don't look back,* she reminded herself. But she couldn't stop herself. When she did glance behind her, she saw them. The same things that attacked that poor boy at school were running hard after them swaying awkwardly like branches being blown in the wind, and they towered over their surroundings. There were at least five of them.

"Hurry, this way!" she said still holding onto Loris' arm. They reached the main road just to realize they had been cornered. As they came out of the alley, they both froze in their tracks. A pack of them were gathered around a dog eating its entrails. Luckily the dog was already dead, but it still broke her heart. She couldn't hold back her emotions, and that was enough to get their attention. The monsters stood and jerked their heads in Loris' and Ellie's direction. The biggest one screeched out as if it was communicating with the pack.

Ellie and Loris were cornered. Ellie grasped Loris' arm tighter, retreating into him and preparing to die.

"Loris, we, I," but before she could finish Loris turned to her,

"Do you trust me?" he asked, his eyes staring directly into hers.

"Yes," she said without hesitation.

He grabbed her hand and led her to the MTR train entrance. It was a bold move, because there could be anything down there, including the monsters, but it was the only choice they had. As they descended the stairs, they glanced back to see the monsters coming toward them picking up speed. This had to work. It just had to. The farther they went down, the darker it got. The power had already been cut. They reached the bottom of the stairs just when the monsters descended on them. They ran to-wards the train platform on the lowest level, but it was almost impossible to see and they were both growing tired. Ellie took out the flashlight she had found at school to see which train platform they were on.

Train to Hong Kong Station.

They had reached the front of the train platform but there was no train and the plastic barrier separating the station from the tracks was still closed.

"Wait, if this is closed, that means nothing is inside yet," Ellie said. "Help me! We have to get it open, quickly!" She clawed at one of the doors prying it open with her bare hands. Some of her fingernails snapped in her desperate attempt and blood trickled out from the force.

"It's not enough pressure," Loris said giving it his best. "We need to find somewhere to hide."

The pounding footsteps of the monsters were getting closer; they couldn't see them yet but they knew they didn't have much time. Loris noticed the rafters on the ceiling and got an idea. "Here, take my hand," he said jumping up and grabbing one of the bars and lifting himself up like he had done this millions of times.

Ellie struggled to pull herself up, even with his help. She was never even able to do a push up, let alone a pull up, though it was on her bucket list.

Loris, realizing she wouldn't make it in time, reached down further and wrapped his arm around her waist, jerking up just enough that she was able to get a hand on the rafter and just in time. But as she stood, she lost her balance and began to fall forward right as the monsters arrived. Such a careless mistake would be the last thing she did, she thought. She just hoped Loris wouldn't be dumb enough to try and save her.

In that moment, time stopped; everything moved slowly, and she felt all of it. She watched their swollen pointed faces search for their prey. They could sense their newest blood bags were nearby. She would fall on top of them, and maybe, if she was lucky, die quickly.

She felt something grab and pull her back in. Before she could react, Loris covered her mouth. She could feel him pressed against her, his heartbeat growing faster with each second that passed. His other hand clenched tightly around her waist. His fingers were digging into her hip.

As the monsters passed by, they sniffed around, jerking their heads in unnatural positions, trying to locate them. Their eyes were bulging out and the veins all over their body were pulsating. They kept screeching to each other, but this was a different frequency than before. They were communicating as they paced back and forth like people do when they're trying to solve a problem. As they made their way across the platform, they tossed trash cans and benches. Their anger was growing.

The expression on the monster's face shared so many similarities to her husband's and his temper. All the awful memories she had tried to suppress of his fits of rage came crashing down. She started hyperventilating so hard that Loris pressed his hand harder to cover her mouth. "Shhh, it's ok," he whispered in her ear. "They're leaving." But she couldn't calm down. She kept gasping for air that she was practically making out with his hand. Just like when she was young, practicing for her first kiss. He grabbed her tighter and she felt something press against her back. Her eyes widened. But she couldn't move yet. Those things were still below them.

After what felt like forever, the monsters finally dispersed. They were in the clear but they stayed still for a while after. Ellie, still in Loris' grasp, turned towards him, placing her hands around his neck to steady herself, their faces inches apart.

He turned away, looking down embarrassed.

"I'm...sorry, I didn't mean to..."

"It's ok," she said.

They both weren't ready for the awkward *sorry I got a boner* talk.

"Thanks for saving me....again," she said taking a seat on the rafters.

"Well, I can't say it wasn't selfish. I'm not about to deal with whatever is happening alone."

"So, what now?" She sat down on the rafters and swung her legs back and forth. They couldn't just stay there. They were sitting ducks.

"Can't go back up. Who knows how many there are now?"

"Wait," Ellie said finally getting an idea, "what if we could find something to pry the platform door open. It'd be safe for us to walk in the tunnels and we'd be able to make it all the way to Hong Kong Station without seeing one of those things."

"That could work, but what happens after?"

"I don't know."

"Let's hope for the best," Loris said helping her down. El took the flashlight back out and handed the second to Loris.

They started to search for anything that would be able to pry the platform doors open. Loris spotted the maintenance room, but it was locked, and they couldn't risk making a lot of noise until they had their way out. Ellie searched a nearby customer service kiosk. The door had been left open. She checked the drawers for keys but didn't have any luck. She noticed a back-pack besides the swivel chair and looked inside. Bingo. They made a great team without even realizing it. Ellie grabbed the keys and handed them to Loris. After trying at least five different keys, they found the right one. Inside they found an old toolbox and grabbed two screwdrivers, a hammer, a wench, and a pliers. They were sure to come in handy. Loris added them to his bag, giving Ellie one of the screwdrivers.

"Just in case," he said.

As they got back to the front of the platform, Ellie kept an eye out while Loris tried to get the doors to the plastic barrier to budge.

"Finally!" he cheered. Ellie turned and saw he had gotten the doors to open.

"Let's go," he said, hurrying her up. He didn't want to spend another minute here.

Ellie jumped down onto the MTR train tracks, repositioning her bag and adjusting her clothes.

"Should we close the barrier door?" she asked. "We should close it, shouldn't we?"

"Good idea. Don't want any of those things getting inside and blindsiding us." They pulled the plastic barrier doors as close together as possible.

They walked through the tunnels with caution, even though they knew they were alone for now.

"Never thought I'd find myself in here," Ellie said, her voice echoing through the tunnels.

"Shit that's loud," Loris commented.

"Funny where life takes us, isn't it?"

"So what do you expect to find once you get home?" Loris asked, kicking rocks. "Are we planning on staying or...?"

"No, there's just something I need," she said keeping her eyes forward. *Closure.*

"Fair enough," he said taking the hint.

For the next few hours, they walked through the tunnels barely saying a word to each other. They were both eager to get out and rest. It was impossible to tell where they were in terms of location or even the time.

"Here," Loris said handing Ellie some water.

"It's alright. We should save it. I'm ok for now." They continued walking when they heard a screeching sound, it sounded like it was coming from a train.

"Hey, I think there's something ahead!" Ellie darted ahead to look. Loris followed quickly behind. He had a bad feeling.

As they got closer to the sound, they saw it. One of the central trains had crashed into another. Cables from the top of the train hung low, exposed. One of the trains was partially inside the other from the looks of it.

They stopped in front of the wreckage.

"I don't understand...what happened?" Ellie said turning to Loris.

"It looks like two of the trains collided. They were both trying to get out," he said. "We have to keep moving." He took a step towards the back of the train. The train doors had all been released open. Someone had pulled the emergency brakes.

"Don't worry," Loris said. "It'll be ok." He tried to reassure Ellie with experience. But this time was different. As they boarded the train and avoided the hanging wires, they immediately covered their mouths. It smelt like rotting meat and death. Ellie horrified at what she saw, couldn't look away. She was reminded of how she wasn't living in a nightmare, that life had become one. There were bodies--families, friends, and lovers, people she saw every day and didn't notice. They were spread out across the train, their decaying faces still showed fear. But it didn't make sense. There never were bodies. There was only evidence of loss. Why were they here? She grasped for answers but couldn't come up with one.

They worked their way through the train, stepping over the dead, acknowledging the horrors with their eyes. They remained speechless until they came upon her, the little girl. She couldn't have been more than four. She wasn't surrounded by anyone. She was there all alone, clutching her Doraemon stuffed toy.

"It's not supposed to be like this," Loris said bending over towards the girl. Tears filled his eyes.

"I know, but it is," Ellie bent down and wrapped her arms around tightly, comforting him. She could feel his breathing getting heavier and more frustrated.

"We need to keep moving Loris," she said pulling him up and continuing forward. He laid a nearby jacket over the little girl.

Once they reached the back of the collided train, they stepped out and saw a platform up ahead. They picked up their pace and hurried to it. They dug into the platform doors to struggle to pry them open. But they slid apart more easily than the ones they had tackled before. As they made their way out, they cautiously climbed to the top level of the MTR station. All was clear so far. They looked at the top of the exits and saw all the clocks. 11:00am. They had been traveling for hours, and it was day. They should be safe for now. They exited the station and headed towards Ellie's home.

Outside the station, it was quiet. No birds, no chaos, just the sounds of their feet on the pavement. Ellie started towards her home when she saw her favorite pastry shop, *Le Cateu*.

"Keep a lookout, Loris, I'll be right back," she said making her way to the shop. The metal gate hadn't been closed all the way. She lifted it up and ventured inside. Most of the bread had already gone stale because it hadn't been stored properly but her favorite hadn't. They must have pumped so many preservatives into the tuna buns but she was thankful for it.

"What'd you get?" Loris said intrigued.

"Dinner," she smiled. Things were going to be ok, she knew it.

"Alright, we're here," she said as they approached her residential building.

"I didn't imagine you living here," Loris commented.

"What does that mean?" She was curious.

"Just pictured you in a more..."

"Posh place?"

"You said it," he laughed.

"Well, you'll come to know a lot of your assumptions are wrong...at least about me."

"What else do you think I assume?" he joked. Ellie laughed and rolled her eyes letting herself in the flat.

The apartment was just as she left it, except for the bedroom. She walked into the bedroom and saw his clothes and bureau drawers spread across the bed and floor. He had left in a panic, packing the essentials which included his passport and all the cash he kept in his underwear drawer. She sat on the bed to take everything in when Loris came in.

"Are you ok?" he asked, sitting beside her. Her eyes puddled with tears. She felt embarrassed about what she was feeling. She wanted him out of her life, and he finally was. But why did she feel this sudden sense of loss? She took a deep breath and tried to smile, but Loris wasn't buying it.

"I can't believe he just left."

"Well he must have heard the alarms and went to the checkpoint with everyone else. Is that why we came here?" he asked.

"What? No, of course not. I just needed..."

"To know?" Loris finished. "I get it, it's ok. I'll be outside." He left the bedroom. As he passed through the living room, he noticed a small folded up piece of paper sitting on the coffee table. He grabbed it on his way out, shoving it into his pocket.

Ellie sat there for a while trying to cope with her feelings. They had all come flooding back, the good and the bad. She had come looking for closure, but it didn't look like she was going to get even that. He was an asshole, sure. But that didn't mean she wanted him dead. She wanted to know he was at least alright despite everything. But he hadn't even left a note. Didn't he have any hope that they'd be reunited again?

As Loris waited for Ellie outside, he walked around her flat, examining the pictures hanging against the walls. To the blind eye, it would appear Ellie had the perfect marriage. But Loris knew better than to base happiness on perception. He stopped when he saw one particular photo. It was of Ellie in a pair of roller skates; she couldn't have been more than six years old. He smiled to himself. She looked so happy there, so innocent and full of life with love to give. He still saw some of those qualities in her. He took the photo out of the frame and placed it in his backpack. Taking a seat on one of the loveseats, he took out the folded piece of paper from the bedroom and started to read it. It was addressed to Ellie.

"What's that?" she said coming out of her room, avoiding her demons.

"Nothing," he said shoving it back in his pocket.

She gave him a suspicious look, but let it go. She was too tired to pry.

"We can stay here for a while," she said to Loris as she walked around the rest of her house, tidying up like it actually mattered. Trying to get back familiar routines and the comforts of being at home.

"Sure, not like we have anywhere else we need to be," he joked.

They grabbed a few essentials from their bags and got comfortable. The hot water was long gone but they were still able to shower and get clean.

"Comfortable?" she asked Loris who was in her husband's pjs.

"As I'll ever be. Is this silk?" he said rubbing his face in the fabric. "It's so soft."

She laughed and started for the living room.

"How 'bout you? What are you wearing?"

"What do you mean?" she was wearing her pjs.

"Oh, my bad, I guess I just always imagined you wearing something a little more..."

"Sexy?"

He shrugged.

"Do you want any tea?"

"I wish, but electricity is out. How are you going to manage that?"

She smiled, "Lavender and lemon it is." She went to her kitchen and turned on the gas burner.

They sat together on the couch, sipping their tea. Ellie gave him the "Condescending Cat" mug while she selected the oversized Robert Frost poetry mug full of clichés. She pulled out her fleece tie-dye floral blanket and wrapped it around herself.

"You *would* have a coffee mug like this," he mocked before taking a sip. "So how does it feel being home?"

"I don't know honestly. Parts of me feel relieved like everything is going to be ok. I'm home, but some parts feel stuck, confused."

"What do you mean?" Loris moved closer.

"It's just funny, you know. I was going to leave him, leave this house and now it's like I couldn't be happier to be here. It feels safe."

"You are safe," he said reassuring her.

"For now, until something happens again, but I'll take it." She raised her mug and took a sip. She was growing pessimistic, a side Loris hadn't seen before.

"Hey, so what did you mean back there when you said your father wouldn't be back?" Ellie asked suddenly shifting the attention from her.

"Trust me, it's a good thing. He never was much of a father to begin with."

"I'm sure he still loved you though in his own way," she tried to comfort him, but he wasn't willing to rehash the past.

"It's fine really. He was dead to me long before any of this happened. It makes no difference whether he is alive or not."

"What about your mother"

"She was dead to me the moment she chose her boyfriend over me. But you know," he said shifting closer to her. "If she had just brought me with her, maybe things would have been different. But she left me... with him. I can't forgive her for that."

"I'm sorry," she said placing her hand on his crossed knee. She knew the feeling of abandonment all too well. When her parents split up neither of them wanted custody, and they didn't even try to hide it from their impressionable daughter.

He placed his hand over hers and looked into her eyes. His eyes kept searching hers for a reaction.

She smiled and tears were starting to build up.

Loris took it as a sign to continue. He placed his other hand on her cheek and started to lean in but Ellie went for a hug instead, moving his hand. They stayed there for a few seconds, but it felt much longer to them. When she pulled back, she couldn't help but smell his hair. It was strangely comforting.

"I'm going to try and get some sleep." She got up and headed to her bedroom. Loris sat back and sighed.
"Ok, goodnight," his eyes followed her till she was out of sight.
"Idiot," he muttered to himself.

DAY 4

The next day, Ellie slept till 3pm. She was exhausted. Loris woke up earlier and decided to cook her eggs and cheese.

"Morning," he said bringing them in with a cup of coffee he brewed.

"Is that coffee?" her eyes opened and lit up immediately. She reached out her hands, caressing the cup as if it were the Holy Grail.

"Made you eggs and cheese too." He placed the plate down beside her with her tuna buns and handed her a fork. They dug in and ate together, avoiding talks of the missed signals from the night before.

"How'd you sleep?" she asked.

"Surprisingly well. I didn't hear any of them last night."

"Same, I just remember I had the most amazing dream," she said trying to recall what it was about.

"Was I in it?" She stared at him awkwardly, eyes growing bigger.

"I'm just kidding, relax," he saved. "So what's the plan?"

"Uhhhh, can we not talk plans for once and pretend everything is normal right now and we're just having a lazy day," she rubbed her eyes.

"So, would you consider me being at your home normal?"

"Do you always have to joke?" she asked.

He did. It's how he dealt with everything.

"Yeah, let's stay here for a few days and regroup."

"So, should we take this time to get to know each other a bit better? I mean all things considering, it's probably good to know what makes you tick." He took a sip of his coffee, watching for her reaction.

Ellie nodded. "What do you want to know? Ask me anything and I'll answer."

He jumped right in it. "How old were you when you first had sex?"

"Really? Come on, Loris!"

"You did say anything and it's not like you're my teacher anymore. So, we can talk about this kind of stuff now." He did have a good point and there wasn't exactly anyone else to talk to about these things and who knew when or if there would be.

"I was seventeen. I was young, stupid, and in love. The perfect combination for disaster."

"I was fourteen." Her eyes widened.

"Fourteen?! I was still playing with Barbie dolls at fourteen." She chuckled.

He remained serious. "Was it everything you thought it would be?"

"No," she said. "It was disappointing."

"Why's that?"

"Because it's not like the movies; it wasn't how I imagined it to be."

"Well, when you build your expectations up and expect reality to measure up to the movies, you're doomed from the start,"

Loris said surprising Ellie.

"Was it everything *you* thought it would be your first time?" she asked.

"More or less. But I think it's a bit different for guys. Once we find out about sex, we have this primal urge to do it as soon as possible, and it doesn't really matter who it's with."

"That doesn't make a difference to you at all?"

"I guess it does a bit. But, I think, the first time, your expectations are different. Girls want it to be with someone they love or at least care about. It's the feeling of intimacy and being wanted, not the act itself. And I think for guys, it's all about becoming a man, being able to do what you've been wanting to from the moment you got your first erection."

"I guess that makes sense. Who was it with? Did you love her?"

"Lauren, the girl we..."

No wonder he was distraught.

"I'm sorry, I..."

"It's ok. It just sort of happened with Lauren one day. I couldn't go home because my father was having one of his fits. He had bet half of his paycheck on the horse races and lost everything. Lauren was there and her parents were both working, and it just happened."

"So were you and Lauren..."

"No, it only happened once. We were just friends, nothing more."

"I meant in love..."

"Have you ever been in love, Ellie?"

"I got married, didn't I?"

"That's not what I asked."

"I thought I was but now I'm not so sure."

Loris didn't push any further, he had read the letter her husband had left for her. He understood why she was having doubts.

DAY 8

They spent the next few nights relaxing and getting to know each other better. They had gone through Ellie's DVD collection, debating the classics of Green Street Hooligans to Snatch—two movies Loris was very familiar with and opinionated about. They played her random assortment of board games between rummaging through pantry cabinets, coming up with bizarre concoctions for dinner. Tonight would be canned peaches and brown sugar.

"These past few days have been..." Ellie started.

"Perfect," Loris finished.

"Yeah, I've barely thought about everything that's been going on outside. You've been a good distraction."

He smiled. "I feel like once you play board games with someone, you really get to know the person too."

"Oh yeah? So, who I am then Loris? What have you learnt?" she asked slyly.

"For one, you're a terrible liar."

"Am not!"

"You do this thing where you bite your bottom lip and try not to look away every time you bluff, but instead your eyes get all bulgy like they're trying to leave your head. It's a dead give-away."

"Do I?" She did it again. No one had ever told her that before. She wanted to go to a mirror and check for herself.

"It's cute."

"What else?"

"You play to win."

"I do what I need to survive. No crime in that," she shrugged.

"But despite your need to win, you still give help, which shows you have a good heart."

"I didn't help you," she protested.

"You don't like to take credit, that's the teacher in you. So how about you? Did you learn anything new in these last few days?" he pressed.

"Just confirmed what I already know."

"And that is?"

"You have a good heart, Loris."

"You're going to have to be a bit more specific." He fished for a compliment.

"You know I'm no good with saying these things."

"Try."

"Ok, well despite everything, you've been there for me in every way. You're so young but you seem to be handling everything with such grace."

"Age has nothing to do with anything."

"That's not what I meant; just I should be the one taking care of you."

"It's not your job to do that. Not just because you're older or that you were my teacher. I can take care of myself, and I told you I'd be there for you. I meant it."

"I know and I trust you with everything."

"Do you trust me with your heart?"

"Loris…"

"I mean everything's different now."

"Not my feelings." She responded instantly.

"Ouch!" His face turned bright red and his eyes widened. He raised his eyebrows and was left speechless. He didn't expect such a quick and brutal rejection. He took some time repositioning himself on the couch.

"Give me some time." She grabbed the plate of peaches and dug in. Juices seeped out and splattered the carpets.

"So where do you think we should go?" she said changing the subject.

"How about the coast? We can get a boat and sail off to one of the outlying islands. Whatever is happening might not have reached there yet."

"That's a nice idea," Ellie said thinking of Lamma Island or Mui Wo as their new home. Their own private island, a fresh start. She hadn't even considered all the current residents of those places that lived there.

"We should start at least making a plan. Just a few days ago we started hearing those things at night wandering around. I think it's time to make a move."

"You're right. We've been here too long already" she agreed.

She grabbed a pen and paper and they started mapping out possible plans.

"So, it's settled. We'll stock up on supplies and then head to the docks," Ellie confirmed.

"We'll leave at dawn."

DAY 9

CHAPTER 13

They set out when the sun had started climbing higher into the sky. Time was insignificant at this point, but it must have been around 6 or 7.

With no more understanding of what was happening around them, Loris and Ellie grew weary, but they still clung onto their hope of finding a boat and escaping this nightmare. It had been days since they had any human contact. A city full of 8 million was now a ghost town.

"So, what's it been? Over a whole week since we've seen another person?" Loris said trying to make conversation as they were walking. He still hadn't realized Ellie was not a morning person.

"I wouldn't say seeing the elderly couple in your building counts as human contact."

He looked back and laughed. She didn't look amused.

"Let's try and go for another few hours if we can. Then we can rest," he said, picking up the pace. She dragged behind, lugging her backpack that was even heavier since leaving home. It was hot and sunny, and there were no clouds in sight or beyond the horizon.

"Hey, check this out," Loris said pointing to an abandoned 7-11. "We could stock up on supplies here since it's not too far from the docks. What do you think?"

"Let's do it," she said. She couldn't wait to be out of the sun. She could feel her skin had already started to burn.

They checked to make sure the coast was clear before making their way inside. Inside everything was still intact; there were no signs of looting.

"Alright, grab anything that looks useful and that isn't too heavy."

"Roger that."

There were no windows in the store except for the front door that they had covered with the pull-down shutter for protection. They had lost track of time stocking up on supplies and didn't notice a storm was brewing.

"Ready?" Loris asked. She nodded. As they opened the shutter to go out, they were met with light rain and the skies had turned black. They both looked at each other confused.

"I don't understand, it was just sunny moments ago... We didn't spend that much time inside, did we?"

Loris confirmed.

Ellie went back inside and grabbed two poncho packs and threw one to Loris, placing hers on and over her backpack. They had to keep moving. They were so close.

"A little rain never stopped anyone," she said venturing out.

As they walked in the middle of the street, getting closer to the docks, they started to hear the screeching sounds they were all too familiar with. It was coming from up ahead but the fog had become too thick for them to see what it was. The sound was growing louder. They proceeded with caution, grabbing each other's' arm for emotional support.

"You don't think that..."

Suddenly, they saw them, a whole pack sniffing around, ravenous like starving dogs spotting their next meal.

"Loris...." her hand slipped down his arm and grabbed his hand. She squeezed tightly.

"Run!" he said pulling her with him as he started to dash off. The fog blinded them in every direction. They couldn't see more than 20 feet in front of them. They could hear the creatures gaining speed and closing in. They were trapped. It was only a matter of time before they'd be ripped apart. They ran into an alley way but at the end was a fence covered in barbed wire. It was locked. They knew they didn't have time to backtrack and get themselves out. Loris stood in front of Ellie still holding her hand.

"What are you doing? We can make it!" she screamed.

He was stared ahead waiting for the monster to emerge from the fog.

"Loris!" she turned him around and slapped him. "We can do this!" she said referring to the fence.

Tears welled in his eyes. She could see he had given up and didn't see a way out of this.

Ellie suddenly started to climb as quick as she could, throwing her backpack over to the other side. The barbed wire was sharp and twisted but she kept climbing and threw herself onto it. She could feel it stabbing into her sides and arms, but she didn't have time to worry about pain. She reached down for Loris' hand.

"Loris!" she yelled down. He was still staring straight ahead at the shapes emerging from the fog. She was desperate to get his attention. He was still in shock.

"Loris!" she pleaded. "Please, I need you!" She reached down as far as she could until she was able to touch his shoulder. He turned around and snapped out of it immediately. He grabbed her hand and pulled himself up and over the fence. He landed on his feet but tripped and fell. Ellie tried to jump down after him, but her shirt was stuck on the wire.

"Fuck!" she screamed. She wasn't about to die this way. She jerked back and forth until it tore, leaving a piece of the fabric on the wire. She helped Loris up and they looked back at the fence. The monsters pushed against the fence trying to break it down. She thought they were safe until the monsters started climbing too. She was in no position to run. She could feel her insides aching and blood leaking out. Her vision was getting blurry.

"Over here!" a woman called out, motioning them to safety. She was hanging out of a window that overlooked a grocery store, waving her hands furiously. Ellie grabbed Loris and sprinted towards the door.

A man was waiting by it with a crowbar. "Hurry," he yelled.

They dashed through the door clumsily, Ellie ramming into a wall. The man pulled the gate down and jammed the crowbar through the lock space. He backed away and within seconds the figures reached the door, banging and scratching violently to get in.

"That was close," the woman from the window said, walking towards them.

"Thanks," they both said in unison, out of breath. Ellie was clutching her sides.

"So, what were you doing out there anyways? Do you have a death wish?"

"It was daytime, why were they out there?!" Ellie asked confused. "I thought they only came out at night."

"Obviously or you wouldn't have been out when they hunt. They don't like sunshine. So they come out during the night and on foggy days when the sun can't reach them regardless of the time. I'm Maya by the way," she said extending her hand.

"Ellie," she said reaching out her blood-stained hand.

Maya examined her hand and turned to Loris.

"Loris," he managed to say though still in shock.

"It's a good thing we saw you when we did. Otherwise who knows what would have happened," she added.

Loris' eyes narrowed and his jaw tightened.

"What happened to your hand?" Maya asked referring to Ellie.

"I hurt myself climbing over barbed wire. Or should I say after throwing myself on to it."

"Impressive." Maya showed her approval. "You did what you had to in order to survive despite the consequences."

Ellie nodded.

"Well, you guys are welcome to stay here for a bit. We've got plenty of food if you haven't noticed," she said spreading out her arms and twirling around. "Just take a look around and grab what you want. We'll be upstairs when you wanna talk. You should get yourself cleaned up; don't want to get an infection," she said leaving with the man.

Ellie wondered why he hadn't introduced himself. But she was just grateful they saw them in time.

"Are you ok?" Loris asked reaching for her hand.

"Yeah, I'll be fine," she pulled away, trying to hide her pain. She didn't convince him.

"I could use a drink though," she said heading straight towards the liquor aisle.

"We deserve a drink after what just happened."

"More than one," she added.

They rummaged through the selection, picking out an aged Nikka Whisky and two bottles of 2011 cabernet sovereign.

"Too bad there isn't any ice."

"But, we can be classy" Ellie said grabbing a box of plastic wine glasses. They both laughed.

They continued shopping for a while until they had gathered what would be their meal for the day. A package of pizza pringles, 5 snickers, two packs of chocolate cake, and a box of Fruit Loops. "Hey, I grabbed some stuff for your hand," Loris handed her some gauze, wrapping tape, and a small bottle of vodka.

"Thanks," she said throwing everything into one of the plastic shopping bags that were still downstairs.

"Let me help," he offered grabbing the bottle of vodka and examining her hand. "It's pretty deep," he said

"Ow!" she pulled her hand back from the stinging pain.

"The worst part is over, you baby," Loris said as he started to wrap her hand up. He did so carefully and gently, paying close attention not to pull too tight. After he finished taping it, he held onto her hand for a moment.

"Thanks for back there."

"It looks like the score is 2 to 1 now. I have to save you one more time for us to be even." She tried to lighten the mood.

She threw the rest of the gauze and wrapping in the bag. She knew she had to deal with the gaping gash in her waist, but didn't want Loris to worry.

"See you found some dinner?" Maya said sitting down in a circle surrounded by four other people.

"Yeah, nothing like a sugar high in these low times," Ellie said. No one laughed. Something she would never get used to.

They joined them on the floor and opened a bottle of wine with some chocolate cake. It was Ellie favorite combo.

"So let me introduce everyone," Maya offered. She seemed to be the one in charge. She couldn't have been more than a few years younger than Ellie.

"This is Moose," she said referring to the guy who has been downstairs earlier.

He nodded, but still didn't speak.

"I'm Joey," a cute girl with pigtails who dressed like she was twelve chirped.

"This here is Tamara, don't fuck with her. She's seen shit," Maya joked. But there was a spooky truth to it. She looked like she had seen things. She was wearing combat boots, cut off jean shorts, and a racerback tee with a sports team logo.

"And, finally, this is Elliot," she pointed to a slightly older Spanish guy around Ellie's age.

"Nice to meet you guys," Ellie said.

"So, how'd you guys come together? Did you know each other before the reckoning or met during?" Elliot asked.

"The reckoning?" Loris asked.

"Yeah, this shit storm that we're currently in, "the reckoning" as we call it. The end of the world, the purge, all answers point to the end of the era of man," he said cryptically.

"Oh, no we knew each other before," Ellie said.

"How?" Joey said.

"We went to school together," Loris chimed in.

Going to school together was one way to put it.

"Oh so you studied together? Which university? I went to City U!" Joey added.

"Baptist," Ellie said. She wasn't sure why she lied. It wasn't necessary.

"No way, so were you there when it happened?" Elliot asked, leaning in closer.

"Yeah, Loris was actually the one who saved me."

Maya and Joey suddenly turned towards Loris in approval.

"Story time!" Joey said clapping her hands.

"It's not so interesting really," Loris said, taking a gulp of the wine.

"Uhm, well, I was upstairs hiding in the dance room when two of those things cornered me. I thought I was going to die, the door behind me was jammed, but then all of a sudden Loris burst in and led me to safety. It all happened so fast."

"Wow, Loris that's amazing. To be there at that exact moment. It's so...."

"Romantic," Joey said, finishing Maya's sentence. She was gleaming into Loris' eyes.

Loris and Ellie took another long sip of their wine, avoiding eye contact with each other.

"It wasn't like that," Loris expressed.

"Yeah, yeah. Anyways, so you've been together ever since? How'd you manage to survive?" Elliot asked, his eyes were still on Ellie.

"We've just kept moving, never staying in one place for too long," Ellie said.

"But you must have some idea of where you're heading," Maya said.

"The coast, it's safe there," Loris said with confidence.

"Yeah, keep that dream alive," Tamara said sarcastically.

"What does that mean?" he asked getting defensive.

"I'm just saying if you can find a safe place, it's better to just stay until you can't, you know? The grass isn't always greener, and this time having that mentality will get you killed."

"Are you speaking from experience then?" Ellie asked, crossing a personal line.

Feeling attacked, Tamara lashed out, "Yeah, that's exactly what happened and why you don't see me smiling anymore," she said getting up and walking out of the room.

"Don't mind her," Maya said, "she's going through some shit."

"Who isn't?" Loris didn't accept her rudeness as an excuse.

Nudging him, Ellie gave Loris a look. The look a mother gives when it's not the time to speak out.

"You guys should get some rest. There's a room upstairs that no one is using you can crash in," Maya offered.

"Thanks," Ellie said getting up.

"Let's talk in the morning," Maya added.

"Night," Elliot said smiling at Ellie. He hadn't taken his eyes off her the whole time she arrived. Even Loris noticed.

Not even a minute had passed when they reached the room that Ellie collapsed onto the bed. It wasn't comfortable but it was better than nothing. Loris took a seat on the edge, taking off his shoes and socks.

"You can take the bed. I'll sleep on the floor."

"Don't be crazy, it's big enough for us both," Ellie said scooting closer to join him.

"Are you sure, I just don't want to overstep," he said looking down.

"Loris, look at me," she said placing her hand on his shoulder, squeezing it slightly.

He turned to look at her.

"After everything we've been through, sleeping in the same bed is nothing," she said.

"El, I, just feel like,"

"You just called me El," she said cutting him off.

"Oh, sorry. I didn't mean…..""No one has ever called me El…It's usually just Ellie, but I like that you do," she said smiling.

"Really?" he asked surprised.

"Of course. Can I ask you something though?"

He nodded.

"Why did you say we went to school together?"

"Well, we did."

"Yeah, but you know what I mean."

"I just…felt embarrassed. Especially around all these people. Telling them that I was your student. And then they said what I did was so romantic. It made me feel… I don't know… I just felt so useless."

"Useless? How can you even say that? You were the one who saved me, Loris! If it wasn't for you, I'd be dead."

"You know what I mean."

"No, I don't, so explain it to me."

"It's just that you're amazing, you do all of these incredible things and know so much about the world and then here I am, the only achievement I have in my life is saving you."

Ellie grabbed Loris' hand and kissed it, pulling him in for a hug.

"Don't you ever say that! You're brave, Loris. Do you know how many people left at the first sign of trouble, some even leaving their family behind? You're my reason for waking up every day. Without you, I probably would've…"

"Would have what?" he said pulling back so he could see her face.

"Ended it a long time ago. I can't do this on my own. You keep me going."

Tears began to form in his eyes, but he blinked them back as best as he could.

"El, I just feel so useless compared to you. Especially after what happened tonight. I froze up; we would have died because I wasn't strong enough. But you carried us both through. You didn't hesitate."

She pulled him back into her embrace. "You're not useless. We're a team."

He held onto her tight and they sat there for a few minutes in silence reveling in the comfort of human contact. But it was interrupted too soon.

"What's that?" Loris looked horrified at the blood that had stained parts of the bed sheets.

She couldn't hide it anymore.

"I'm fine, I just cut myself on my sides a bit from the barbed wire," she tried to downplay her pain, but he wasn't buying it.

"El, it looks serious. Let me see." She headed to the bathroom mirror and tried to remove her shirt, but it was stuck to her. She let out a sigh of pain.

"Let me help," he said turning on the shower and grabbing the head. "It needs to be wet or it'll rip the skin when you take your shirt off."

She got in the shower and he ran the shower head over the bottom half of her shirt, trying not to get the lower half of her body or her hand wet in the process. The water was freezing.

"Here" He gave her a towel to wrap herself with. He started to cut the shirt with a pair of scissors he grabbed from his backpack. Halfway through cutting, he began to see how serious the cuts were.

"How does it look?" she asked already knowing the answer from the pain she was in.

"It looks bad, El. Why didn't you say something earlier?" he said noticing her bra was visible for a moment before looking away.

"I didn't want you to worry."

"You can't keep things like this from me. We're supposed to be a team remember? Don't hide things on account of being afraid they'll upset me."

"I'm sorry," she said genuinely.

"We need to see how deep it goes; you might need stitches."

She grimaced. "We don't have supplies like that. You'll have to glue it."

"With superglue? Are you kidding?"

"It'll work, at least temporarily until we can find something else. I have some in my bag."

He wanted to argue, but there wasn't any other option. After he cleaned out her wound, he got the glue ready.

"I'm gonna need your help," he said. "You're going to have to stay still; you can't move, ok?"

She nodded.

"When I put the glue on, I need you to hold it tight, ok? Make sure your hand doesn't get any of the glue on it or we'll be in a whole 'nother mess."

"I'm ready."

He counted down starting at three, but at two he applied the glue and they both put pressure on the tears in her skin. It wasn't an intimate moment, but it felt personal as they were both looking with such intensity at each other.

After about five minutes, they both released their hands, and Loris wrapped her up.

"You need to rest more, and don't do anything that is going to cause it to rip back open."

"Thanks," she grabbed an oversized t-shirt out of her bag and placed it on the bed.

"Can you help me? I can't really reach my arms up right now."

Loris walked over to her and grabbed the shirt.

"Sorry, can you help me with this too," she asked shyly referring to her bra. It was already difficult enough with two hands to un-latch it; it was impossible now.

"Of course," he tried to hide the nervousness in his voice.

He slowly unlatched the bra from the back, and it fell onto the floor in front of her as he brushed it off her shoulders. He stood for a moment, his hand lingering on her shoulder, admiring all the curves and freckles on her back. She didn't tell him off.

He grabbed the t-shirt and pulled it over her head and through her arms, brushing the uninjured side of her waist, feeling how tiny it was. She sat down on the bed and he then proceeded to help her with her pants, kneeling down, pulling each leg out. He was so close to her. He wanted more.

"Do you need anything else?" he asked placing her clothes on the dresser.

"Think I'm alright, thanks," she smiled and retreated under the covers.

He sat on the edge of the bed facing her.

"Aren't you coming?" she asked referring to bed. She pulled open the covers and patted the side. He came closer and got in.

Trying to get comfortable, she turned onto her good side and was facing Loris now.

"Sweet dreams," she whispered. He kissed her forehead and dozed off. They were both exhausted. But El couldn't pass out as quickly as he had. She could feel his breath on her face. She watched him quietly, observing all of the lines and scars that graced his face. A piece of hair had fallen over his forehead and she brushed it back behind his ear softly. She scooted her head closer until their noses were practically touching. In fact, they were. But she felt a familiar comfort and didn't pull back. It was innocent and he was asleep. Only she would know.

She could hear the laughter of everyone below. She wished she could be so light-hearted at a time like this and enjoy herself. But she was still struggling to come to terms with everything changing and how she was feeling now. She didn't know what it meant.

That night, Ellie dreamt of having her old life back but in this version, Loris wasn't her student, they had met in different circumstances. They didn't have a complicated past. The weight of the world wasn't upon them. It wasn't all or nothing; there was no risk that would put her career and reputation in jeopardy. Instead, they sat on swings by the beach and drank Dirty Shirlies followed by midnight strip teases by bonfires and moonlit skinny dip swims. It was paradise. But it was over too fast. She felt reality creeping in, clawing at her, and dragging her back to a horrifying reality.

DAY 10

CHAPTER 14

She opened her eyes to be met with Loris staring right back. They were still in the same position, their noses still touching, like Eskimo kisses. How long had he been watching her? Her leg had somehow wrapped around his body while she was sleeping, and it was still there. He was pulled close like a lover. She could feel his heartbeat in his lower region. His hand was on the low of her back, wrapping around to her waist.

"Do you always watch people sleep?" she said repositioning herself turning onto her back.

"Never gotten the chance before," he said reminding her of his age. "Did you sleep well?"

"Yeah, why do you ask?"

"I've just never seen someone smile so much while they were sleeping. Didn't even know that's a thing."

"I was smiling?" she asks sitting up and crossing her legs.

"And you kept talking. It's what woke me up," he said.

"Oh God, what did I say," she thought. She remembered her not so innocent sexy dream immediately.

Loris, sensing she was embarrassed, let up a little.

"Oh, nothing much, except that you kept calling out my name. Loris! Loris!"

El, turned to Loris with her mouth wide open. "Liar!" she said, chucking a pillow at him.

"Nah, you didn't, but a guy can dream right?"

"Is that what you dream of then?" she retaliated.

Relieved he was just kidding, she laid back down, cuddling the pillow.

"I don't want to leave."

"You're telling me you want to stay with some strangers instead of it just being us?"

"No, I mean bed; I don't want to get out of bed today," she clarified, unwrapping a Snickers.

He laid back down too, turning towards her.

"Yeah I could get used to waking up to this view every morning," he said.

"Is there an off switch to your charm? You might as well give up, it's not happening."

"Come on, you love it."

"True."

They both started laughing as if they had been the type of friends who had inside jokes.

"You guys up?" a voice yelled from behind the door. It was Maya.

"Yeah, we'll be down in 5," Ellie said. The footsteps disappeared.

"Guess it's time to face the world," Loris said throwing on his shirt. He helped Ellie get dressed.

As they made their way downstairs, the smell of coffee greeted them. Ellie immediately lit up.

"Morning," Elliot said, handing Ellie a cup of coffee while ignoring Loris. Ellie smiled and took a sip, then passed it to Loris who grabbed the cup and eyed Elliot.

"You guys sleep well? It sure sounded like it," Maya chuckled.

"El cut herself up pretty deep; we were sewing her up" Loris defended.

"That's a relief," otherwise I'd be jealous," Elliot said, smiling at El.

Loris moved closer to her.

"So, here's the deal," Maya got straight to it. "If you wanna stay here, that's great. But you gotta help out. We all contribute here."

"Sounds fair," Ellie said.

"Not sure how long we're staying though," Loris interjected.

"That's fine, but as long as you're here, you can help us hunt."

"Hunt what? Animals? It looks like there's enough food here to last months."

"The dead ones, that's what we call them," Tamara came in.

"And how do we do that? All we know is that they hunt us for no reason," El said.

"We'll tell you what we know and in exchange, you help us trap one, deal?" Maya suggested.

"Alright."

They sat around a table and were briefed by Maya and Tamara about 'the dead ones.' It turns out they had both had near death experiences with them before, Tamara being more personally afflicted than Maya.

"So, I was at the cinema when it happened. My boyfriend and I were on a double date with two of our friends. Horror flick, you know, we wanted to feel scared. But about halfway through, we started hearing screams. At first, we thought it was coming from the movie, but before we could realize what was happening, they infiltrated the theatre. We were sitting up in

115

the back, next to the projection room, and we saw it happen like it was a movie. People were running towards the exits, but they were everywhere. They just started attacking people, lunging on them, and ripping into their chests. We saw a four-year-old girl get dismembered in front of her parents, we realized how fucked we were. It was a bloodbath. We were frozen in our chairs. I remember my nails were digging into my boyfriend's palm. Within moments, they were making their way up towards us. Our two friends had already started running to try and get into the projection room; it was the only way out. We started dashing towards it, but my friend Samantha saw the dead ones getting closer and she panicked. She locked the door behind them and stepped away. I pounded on the door, begging her to let us in, but she just backed away into the wall saying how sorry she was. Her boyfriend held her and looked away. He wasn't prepared or man enough to watch his best friend get ripped apart. He was a fucking coward."

Tears started rolling down her face, she kept choking them back and continued.

"Realizing they weren't going to open the door, my boyfriend grabbed me and kissed me hard. It was the longest and shortest kiss of my life. I knew he was saying goodbye. But I didn't really know, you know? You always think you'll both make it out of the situation somehow, but it wasn't like that. When the dead ones finally reached us, my boyfriend shielded me from them and looked back one last time. He didn't need to say it, but I knew he loved me. He took out his pocketknife and charged towards them, stabbing one in the head. But it didn't stop it. It didn't work like it did in the movies. I don't know how I got out, but I just knew I needed to run. And I did, I ran out of the theatre and kept running, never stopping anywhere for longer than a few hours. And then Maya found me."

Maya rubbed her shoulder and took over. Ellie and Loris couldn't find the right words to express their sympathy.

"So, stabbing them in the head doesn't work like you would think it would," Maya came in.

"Do you have any theories?" Ellie asked.

"We're working on it."

"I noticed that they're never out during the day, why is that?" Loris asked.

"Don't know, but it's our chance to gain the advantage. If we can find out where they go or hide, maybe we can trap one of them and find out more about them," Maya said with determination.

"Where to even start though? We've been traveling for so long, and they don't leave any trace behind," Ellie questioned.

"You said you saw a student get killed by one?" Maya turned to Ellie.

"Yeah but I didn't stick around to see what happened and by the next day, the only evidence of what had happened was blood stained tiles."

"No body, they just...disappear into thin air. There's no explanation," Tamara said frustrated.

"So our only option is to capture one at night or follow one and see where they go."

"Have you guys tried to do this before?" Loris asked.

"No, but we have the numbers now, that is, if you guys are willing to help,"

Maya said, clenching her jaw, hoping to hear what she wanted.

"Of course, they'll help, where else are they going to go?" Elliot said barging into the conversation, taking charge.

Ellie looked at Loris and they exchanged inner dialogues. They knew they needed to stay for a little longer, at least until they understood what exactly they were up against. They needed to survive, and this was the smartest option.

As lunch drew near, Elliot laid out a map of his plans, showing them both what he had in store for the night. There were markings all over the alleyways and weird symbols drawn and circled on the bottom.

"What do these mean?" Loris said pointing to the symbols.

"You wouldn't get it," Elliot belittled.

"I think if we're going to be helping you, we'd better know what they mean," Loris furrowed his brow.

"Relax, they don't have any special or secret meaning. They're just reminders for me. Think of them as mnemonic devices. Don't worry, I'll explain everything."

Ellie cut in to diffuse the growing tension, "So, what's the plan?"

"So, here's where we'll camp out and wait. Usually they come in packs, never alone, so we'll have to isolate one somehow. Any ideas?" he says looking at them both.

"We could distract them and then grab the straggler," Loris suggests.

"Only the others would catch on and within seconds we'd be dead. We have to outsmart them. They're predators by nature, but we have the advantage."

"And what advantage is that?" Ellie asked confused. She couldn't think of a single one.

"We have each other and that gives us something to live for," Elliot says looking at her with desire in his eyes. But Ellie didn't notice his flirtatious comment.

Loris rolled his eyes. *How could this guy be serious?*

"Having people you love in your life isn't an advantage; it's a weakness. At least if you're alone, you don't have anything left to lose," Tamara says joining in.

"Keep telling yourself that," Elliot said dismissing Tamara.

"What if we set a trap to catch one? That way they'd be alone, and we wouldn't have to put ourselves in danger going out at night," Ellie says. Everyone turned to look at her immediately.

"That's...actually not a bad idea," Maya said in approval.

"So it's agreed then?" Elliot confirmed.

"Let's get started then," Maya smiled.

DAY 20

For the next few days, they worked effortlessly on their plan, making sure they had covered all options and scenarios, including the improbable and impossible ones. Ellie and Loris had grown closer over the days and their relationship seemed to be evolving. It no longer felt like a student-teacher relationship but a veteran friendship.

When the day finally came, everyone was feeling quite optimistic. They had done test trials in the apartment and, with a few setbacks, they were able to fix the minor details.

"Hey, come over here and check this out," Loris said to Ellie.

She scurried over.

"So, I think I've finally worked it all out." He grabbed his schematics to unveil the plan. Elliot turned out to be more talk than anything else. His ideas failed the test run and even he couldn't deny Loris had outdone himself.

"So, the dead ones travel in groups the moment the sun is gone, so we'll go set the traps before it gets dark and come back at first light. There's an area close by that is under construction, so if we can manage to cover the ditch with something, the dead ones will walk right on it and fall through." Ellie started to smile.

"We'll put sharpened sticks or gather whatever we can to stick into the bottom of the hole so when they fall, they'll be impaled. Then, in the morning we'll come and collect one."

Elliot stepped in, "That won't work. We'll get bitten for sure!"

Loris grinned. "Which brings me to the next part. We'll use a three-holed noose to pull them up by their arms and neck and once we get them out; we'll use the rest of the rope to secure them."

"Only one problem. How are we going to get them to walk over the trap?" Elliot added.

"We make noise, lots of it," Ellie chimed in. "I used to make wind chimes with my mom when I was young with seashells and sea glass we'd collect from the beach. Every time the wind blew, it'd sing to us, calling us to listen to its song," Ellie said grabbing things around her. "We can use beer cans and fill them with coins or whatever we can find. That way we don't need to be there."

It was the first time Loris heard Ellie talk about her mom.

"And how can you be sure it's going to be windy?" Elliot inquired.

"I always know when a storm is coming. Ever since I was little, I would always get this uneasy feeling in my chest right before a storm" Ellie added, looking up at him, daring him to keep questioning her. "My mom called it a sixth sense," she laughed.

"I like that," he flirted, taking his leave.

Loris turned to Ellie and thanked her for supporting him.

"Looks like we're going to need a lot of beer cans. Get ready to drink," he joked, walking away to join the others.

As they gathered and prepared for the long day ahead, Loris and Ellie felt hopeful, felt like they might be able come out on top after all they had been through. Loris and Elliot brought up a few 30 pack cases of beer, and they all spent the rest of the afternoon chugging beers to assemble their DIY wind chimes. By the time they had all finished, it was half past five and the sun was already setting. They'd have to wait a little longer to set up the traps. Ellie and Loris were comfortable with that. And judging by all the wind chimes they had managed to make, so was the rest of the group. Maya stood up to address the group.

"Guys, I think we have a real shot at this, and I just want to say thanks. It hasn't been easy but we're getting by," she said paying special attention to Moose and Tamara.

Moose lifted his chin up and nodded; he still hadn't spoken. Tamara smiled, looking down.

"I say for tonight, let's just try and pretend it's just another night. Let's pretend that these things aren't out there waiting for us. Let's just have fun and celebrate us finally making a plan," she said tossing Loris a beer.

"Fun… I don't even know what that word means anymore," Tamara said, grabbing one for herself, chugging it straight away, and her eyes off in space. Moose joined in.

"That's what I'm talking about!" Joey squealed excitedly. She had been waiting to relive her party days in the clubbing district of Lan Kwai Fong.

"Everyone, go get ready and meet back here in an hour. Go all out like it's your last night," Maya said flicking her hair back.

Closing the door to the room, Loris sprawled out onto the bed.

"Go all out, ha. You think she was serious?" he asked.

"Well I don't know about you, but I'd like to feel pretty for a change," Ellie said patting her face while looking in the mirror. Looking beautiful was a luxury now.

"You always look pretty," he said.

She gave him that look—the look when a man says something but doesn't really mean it.

"Yeah, but I want to really feel it, you know? I haven't felt like that in so long.."

"Since this started?" he got up and was now standing behind her.

"Honestly, it was probably before I married my husband," she let it slip out. It was too personal.

"How can I help?" he was inches away.

"Just be here. I'm going to go downstairs and try and find some makeup and freshen up," she said smiling. She had a glow in her eyes as she left.

Grabbing a basket, she made her way right to the makeup aisle, wasting no time. Looking at the shelves, it was just another ordinary day. Elf cosmetics and Kiko stood out to her from all the rest; they were after all, cruelty-free. She grabbed the velvet crush black eyeliner, volumizing mascara and finally, her signature red velveteen lipstick. Her face was that of porcelain already, so she didn't bother with cover up. She didn't need it. She grabbed a can of brand-name hair spray and was about to head back when something caught her eye. Daisy, her favorite perfume, just sitting right there on the top shelf. She used to spritz it on three times a day as part of her daily routine. It reminded her of floral patterns, sweetness, and the sun. She grabbed it and put in the basket. Before leaving, she turned back and grabbed a cologne she would later give to Loris.

"It's funny how we still cling to our old rituals," Tamara said looking at the basket.

"What was yours?" Ellie engaged.

"Never was one for makeup," she said taking a sip of the beer. Ellie was trying to think of something to say when Joey popped in.

"Ellie! You have to let me do your makeup!"

"That's alright, I think I got it covered," she said trying to be polite.

"Come on! How often does this happen? It's not like Maya or Tamara are into this sort of thing," she looked at Ellie with puppy eyes.

Ellie never could say no, "I guess if it'll make you happy" she said already getting pulled away by Joey.

Tamara rolled her eyes and muttered something to herself.

"Ok, so tell me, what do you think of Elliot," Joey asked while teasing Ellie's hair.

"Yeah, he seems fine."

"I mean, he obviously has a thing for you. Every time you're both in the same room, he can't take his eyes off you," she said pulling tighter.

"Ow," Ellie cried out. "I mean, yeah, I noticed him looking at me, but I didn't think anything of it."

"He's clearly into you, I mean he has never looked at me or anyone else like that. It's hard enough to even hold his attention. He's so stuck up!"

Ellie nodded.

"You should have fun tonight. I mean who knows what's going to happen tomorrow. You only live once right?" Joey, the girl full of clichés, had a good heart.

"Honestly, Elliot isn't my type."

"What do you mean? With this situation, you can't be too picky!"

"As you said, he seems stuck up."

"How 'bout Loris? It seems like you two got chemistry," she noted.

Ellie immediately got defensive.

"Of course not! It's not like that."

"Woah! Ok, ok chill. So, does that mean he's available then?" Joey showed interest.

"It's complicated. We're friends. Anyway, it would never work," she said trying to convince herself.

"If you say so…" Joey wasn't as convinced.

"Viola! You look beautiful, no fierce even! A force to be reckoned with!" Joey said applying her finishing touches to Ellie.

Ellie looked in the mirror and smiled. She did well.

"Regardless of if you find Elliot attractive or not, it's always nice to just have someone you know? Especially in times like these," Joey said as she started to apply her own makeup.

She was right to a certain extent, but it wasn't Elliot she was thinking about.

She grabbed the rest of her makeup and headed back up to the room where Loris was waiting.

CHAPTER 15

She felt nervous for some reason. It was silly, she thought, being nervous about seeing Loris. Nothing had changed or was different between them, except that she was vulnerable for the first time in a while. Old insecurities surfaced. Every time she made an effort to look nice, her husband would berate her and put her down. It wasn't fair to compare Loris to him.

She closed the door to the room and noticed Loris was in the shower. Great, it would give her time to put her stuff away and get composed. She sat on the edge of the bed, took out her notebook and started documenting the past few weeks. She had been slacking on writing ever since it started.

"Woah, you look amazing, and that smell—it smells like sunshine in here," Loris said walking out of the bathroom with a towel tied around his waist. Ellie couldn't help but stare at his bare chest. He looked stronger and more defined than before.

"Thanks, it's my favorite. Here I got you something too," she said handing him the cologne she picked out.

"I've never worn anything like this before. My dad always wore his Old Spice, but it smelt like aging." He took the bottle and sprayed a few clicks onto his chest.

"How do I smell?" he joked.

Ellie breathed in and smiled. "Like heaven."

Loris threw on a plain black v-cut shirt and jeans. His hair had started to air dry.

"Here," she said handing him a plastic wine glass filled to the brim.

"Going hard already?" he teased.

"I mean, why not?" She raised her glass and they toasted.

"All things considering El, I'm happy I get to spend this night with you."

"Me too," she said, being reminded of what Joey said.

"Guess we should head down, huh?"

"Guess so," she said half-heartedly.

"Took you guys long enough!" Maya said calling them out.

"You did say go all out. Perfection takes time," Ellie bantered.

Elliot and the others were already seated in a circle on the floor sipping on their concoctions. From the smell of it, they were loaded with alcohol and skimmed out on the juice.

Elliot looked at Ellie in awe while Joey did the same to Loris.

"Sit next to me, Loris," Joey said patting the spot next to her. Loris half-smiled, he was too focused on noticing the way Elliot was staring at Ellie.

They both sat down, cupping their drinks.

"So, where were we then?" Maya said regrouping. "Ah, yes, we were sharing our most intimate moments with each other. I mean what better way to get to know someone, especially the people you're counting on to survive. Am I right?"

They both took a sip of their drink.

"How about we up the antics and play some good ol' fashioned truth or dare?" Joey suggested. She looked at Loris and blushed.

"Truth or dare? You serious? That's a game for kids, Jo." Tamara shut her down.

"Oh, come on Tamara, it'll be fun, you'll see. Maybe it'll finally give you the chance to kiss Moose."

Tamara gave Joey the evil eye. She had gone too far.

"Alright, you really want to play Jo, truth or dare?"

"What makes the game interesting is that the person who finishes their drink first and flips over their cup gets to ask the slowest person a question," Joey raised her brow. "And I always win," she said confidently.

"You're on," Tamara said raising her glass. Joey passed out the rest of the solo cups with a mysterious liquid inside. It smelled stronger than rubbing alcohol.

"I'm not even going to ask what's in this," Loris said suspiciously.

"Better not to," Joey smirked.

"Ok, on the count of three. One, two, three!" Everyone started to down their drink. Ellie spit it out immediately, not expecting the sour taste. Elliot flipped his cup first, and turned to Ellie. She had lost.

"Interesting," Joey said, pushing Elliot on Ellie again. She couldn't take a hint.

"El, truth or dare," he asked coyly.

"Truth," she replied.

"Who's the most handsome person in the room, in your opinion, of course," he smiled deviously.

Everyone got silent and turned to Ellie. "That's really your first question?" she asked, trying to buy herself some time. She knew the answer, but it wasn't as easy to say it.

"Ok, if you had to choose one person in this room to spend the night with, who would it be? Is that better? Just trying to gauge if I have a shot," he winked.

"I'm married," she said, coming to her own rescue. She thought she had handled it well.

"That's not what I asked," Elliot said raising a brow. "If you don't answer, you have to chug a cup."

"Fair enough," she filled up her cup and drank.

"You're no fun," Joey teased.

They kept going. The dares ranged from drunken kisses to taking off articles of clothing. Almost everyone was missing their shirts now. It was Maya's turn to ask Loris. He chose dare.

"I dare you to kiss Joey," Maya said sensing Joey's crush. They both were pretty drunk. Loris leaned in quickly, planted a slobbery kiss on Joey's mouth, and pulled back looking directly at El. She turned away.

"Come on people! Your dares are so boring!" Tamara complained. "If you want to kiss, just do it. You don't need to be dared to get the courage." Elliot turned to Ellie and winked.

"El, truth or dare?" Elliot asked.

"Dare."

"I dare you to kiss me." Ellie scooted over to him when he added, "And mean it. I mean really mean it. I want you to want this."

Ellie leaned over and closed her eyes, the whole world was spinning around her. She had lost one too many times. She fell onto his face. Everyone started laughing but Elliot kept trying to make his way in. He looked so sleazy.

"Ok, ok that's enough," Tamara pulled him away.

Elliot pushed her back annoyed.

It was Loris' turn.

"Have you ever been in love?" Tamara asked, curiously.

Everyone got silent and turned to Loris.

"Yeah, I have."

Ellie was still dizzy and recovering, but she was still lucid enough to hear his answer. She wondered if it was Lauren. She had this delusion that it could be her.

"With who?" Joey asked.

"I answered the question already," Loris ended.

Ellie couldn't keep her eyes open any longer. Her tolerance for alcohol had dropped significantly.

"Think it's time for us to call it a night," Loris said helping Ellie to her feet.

Elliot stood up. "I can help," he said.

Loris pulled Ellie closer.

"Stay Loris!" Joey said grabbing his arm and trying to pull him down. He turned and shook her off, but she wasn't getting it. He finally got free from her grasp but when he looked back, Elliot was already leading Ellie back to the room.

Elliot had his arm placed around Ellie's waist and was too close for comfort. In the corridor, he pushed her up against a wall and started kissing her neck and placed his hand underneath her shirt.

"Stop..." she protested, but she didn't have the strength to fight him off.

"Come on, El, how long has it been?" He tried to convince her. "I can make you feel good."

Suddenly Loris came around the corner and pushed him off.

"She needs a man, not a boy," Elliot sneered.

"You're not a man," Ellie said, opening her eyes. The whole thing seemed to sober her up.

Elliot sneered and stormed off.

"You ok?" Loris asked, opening the door to their room.

"Why did you kiss Joey?" she asked. She hadn't sobered up as much as he had thought.

"It was a dare. Come on El, you kissed someone too."

"Yeah, but it's different, I didn't want to."

"You think I wanted to kiss Joey?"

"I don't know what you want."

She slumped onto the bed and reached out her arms.

"Loris! Tuck me in!" She was acting like a child.

Loris leaned down and pulled the covers up around her. He leaned over and kissed her on the cheek.

She turned her head and met his lips, pulling him in closer, wrapping her hands around his head. It was their first kiss. He didn't resist, his lips pushed back and they lingered for a few short moments that felt like eternity. He crawled under the covers and held her tight. He was terrified that she wouldn't remember tomorrow. He was equally terrified she would.

"Good night," she said clutching her pillow.

DAY 21

CHAPTER 16

The next morning, grunts and retching were heard all around. Turns out Ellie wasn't the only one who got completely hammered. Luckily they still had a few days before they were supposed to go set up the traps and carry out their mission. Everyone was preoccupied clutching bins and toilets.

"Morning," Ellie said turning to Loris. She didn't give any indication that she had remembered last night. But she did.

"Hey, how you feeling?" Loris asked, bringing her some water.

"Like hell," she laughed. "We went pretty hard last night, huh?"

"Do you remember everything?" he pushed, looking for any indicator that she had remembered the kiss.

"Yeah, I remember everything, I think," again giving no indicator.

"Should we go find the others?"

"After last night, I really don't want to see Elliot."

"Don't worry, I won't let him near you."

"I can handle it, but thanks."

They got somewhat presentable and went down.

"You guys look like shit," Tamara said as they walked down and joined everyone. It was a room full of panda eyes and tangled hair.

"First to retire and last to reemerge. Good night," Maya implied.

"So, what's the plan?" Ellie asked.

"We take the next few days to go through our plan one last time and make sure we haven't missed anything. We'll set up the traps in the next few days. Let's regain our strength first," Maya instructed.

Elliot barged in. "Morning Ellie," he said with a somewhat hostile tone, not making eye contact.

Ellie ignored him and turned towards the others. "Let's get to it."

DAY 27

Over the next few days, Ellie and Loris stuck close to each other and continued to run through the plans.

"Ok, we leave in 10 to set up the traps," Maya announced. Today was the day.

"You heard 'em, we grab everything and get it done quickly," Tamara said.

"Alright, let's do this then," Loris said.

They grabbed the supplies and made their way outside. It was sunny and the weather had gotten warmer. They split up; Tamara and Moose set out west to secure the perimeter and render supplies for containing the dead one they would hopefully catch while Maya, Joey, Elliot, Ellie, and Loris set out east to set up the traps.

"Do you really think this is going to work?" Joey asked, not confident.

"It will as long as we don't half-ass anything. Have some faith," Maya said.

"Of course, it will," Elliot said. "It was my idea. I designed it after all."

"You mean Loris' idea?" Ellie butted in.

"Whatever... it was a team effort."

They got to the ditch and set up the wooden bamboo that had been sharpened into spikes at the bottom and hung the wind chimes overhead. They covered the hole with bamboo rods that were previously used for construction and patches of fake grass they had found from a nearby park. Luckily enough, there was enough to be able to stretch across the hole without looking suspicious. Many hours had passed and they were growing anxious.

"I think this is gonna work. It could fool me, especially in the dark," Loris approved.

Ellie smiled in approval. "Let's hope so. It's starting to get dark, we should head back," Ellie said.

"This will work," Maya said.

"It will, it has to," Elliot said determined. Failure was not an option.

They all headed back and met up with Tamara and Moose who were already back.

"Finished?" Tamara asked without looking up. She was tying a set of ropes in intricate knots for confinement. Ellie was immediately reminded of her husband's darker side. All of his kinks.

"Take a look at this," Tamara motioned for them to come over. Moose bent over next to her, securing metal rods together that formed a small box. It was designed to be a puzzle only he knew how to open.

"Once we catch one of them, we'll place it in here. There's no way to get out," Tamara said confidently, smiling proudly at Moose. Moose's face was still serious and he still hadn't talked. *What was his story?* Ellie wanted to ask but she didn't want to intrude.

"Now, we wait," Maya said staking out. "We'll be positioned around the trap, hiding in the crevices of the buildings up above. We'll be able to see what happens in real time. We'll split up; Tamara and Moose will go together, then Joey and I, Ellie and

Loris and finally Elliot, you'll be fine on your own, right?" she didn't give him a chance to respond.

Everyone went out and found a building ledge to wait on. They had a long night ahead of them. The anticipation kept their adrenaline up. Ellie and Loris hid in the barred window of an old building; they were alone again.

"Hope this works," Ellie said. "It'd be nice to finally know what we're dealing with."

"It will; have some faith."

"In God? Don't tell me you're religious."

"I mean have faith in us."

Ellie felt stupid now. "Of course I do, sorry. I'm just stressed. The sun has started to go down."

"I know, but it means we're closer to finding out how to end this. I'll keep watch," Loris said.

Ellie leaned her head on his shoulder and closed her eyes. "You're the best."

"Yeah, I know," he said, reminding her of the old Loris, the confident and carefree one.

About an hour later, it was pitch black and sounds of the darkness started to emerge. Ellie was awakened by a loud crash and screeching. It seemed their trap had worked. The screeching grew louder. Ellie didn't dare to look out the window. Loris' eyes were glued to it and she could see his horror.

"Loris…"

He didn't respond.

Ellie slowly turned and glanced towards the window. She saw a dead one squealing and squirming trying to get free. It had fallen on one of the spiked bamboo pieces. It was sticking right through the place where a heart should be. It should be dead. At least now they knew the dead ones anatomy wasn't the same as humans.

Ellie and Loris stared out the window looking around for the others. They must have heard the screeching. It was deafening being so close and hearing it. It was hard to stay quiet and not scream your lungs out in fear. A few moments later a few more dead ones emerged from the dark shadows. They walked in a different formation than usual. They weren't walking as hunters but approaching at a much slower pace. There were five of them in total—all huddled around the hole that one had fallen through. They started communicating with each other in clicks and then looked around the area, scanning the perimeter. Loris and Ellie clutched the edges of the window, being careful not to be spotted.

A few moments later, they were distracted by the sounds of footsteps—footsteps that must have been oblivious and un-aware of the dangers around them. The figures immediately changed their posture, hunching their backs, and their nails became claws lashing out. It wasn't moments later that they heard the screams coming from the other side of the building. Loris and Ellie ran to the window on the other side and saw a young couple with backpacks. The man was already pinned to the ground. Three of the dead ones were crouched around him, tearing him apart. The biggest of the three cupped his hands into the chest and drew out blood, drinking it while the others took bites. His whole body was twitching until it wasn't. The other two were chasing the girl. She was between a car and a small shop. She weighed both her options before running to-wards the store, hoping the door would be unlocked, it wasn't. They jumped on her and one went straight for her neck, ending it quickly. They feasted for what felt like forever. Ellie and Loris couldn't take their eyes off of it. After a while, they both grew numb, feeling nothing for the two victims that were outside. The only thing they felt was relief that it wasn't them. After-wards, the figures stood up and moved on, leaving their cap-tured comrade behind. I guess they didn't do "loose ties."

That's when Loris and Ellie noticed the bodies; they started evaporating into thin air, leaving behind only carnage and blood. They finally knew what happened to all of the victims' bodies.

"This makes no sense. Where are they going? How is this even possible?" Ellie tried to wrap her head around what she had just witnessed.

"I have no idea," Loris was just as puzzled.

They continued to camp out for the night, being careful not to make any noise. The dead ones had moved on to their next victim but they didn't want to risk being exposed.

The sun had started to slowly rise which brought relief to Loris and Ellie but they still had to get to the dead one they trapped before it disappeared. Before Loris and Ellie left the window, they saw Tamara and Moose emerge, walking carefully to the edge with their ropes and weapons. They were prepared. Elliot was next, but he didn't get as close. Maya and Joey were standing behind everyone while Loris and Ellie walked towards them.

"It bleeds," Tamara said, referring to the puddle of blood that was piling up at the bottom.

"The blood is a blackish blue," she continued.

"So how are we going to get it up; it's not moving now," Ellie asked.

"Let's hope it stays that way," Maya said gravely.

"We use these ropes as a pulley and tie them around each limb and pull it up," Tamara said well-aware of the dangers.

"No one said we'd have to get in the pit with it!" Joey said frightened. She hadn't signed up for this. No one had.

"How else did you think we were going to get it out?" Tamara demanded. "Are you that delusional? Anyways, me and Moose will go down. I'll need the rest of you to pull the ropes up.

Understood? And do it quietly! We don't know if any more are nearby. Keep a lookout."

Everyone nodded. Without hesitation, she and Moose climbed down swiftly. Their arm muscles bulged; they must have been rock climbers before. They knew exactly where to place their hands and feet. Once they were down, they approached the dead one carefully, it still wasn't moving. They needed to act fast. They tied the ropes around its hands and feet and queued for the group to start pulling it up. They would need to help un-impale it. The group started to pull, and Moose placed his hands under its backside pushing up. His hands were covered in a slippery, slime-like substance. It smelt foul. Tamara tied a rope around its mouth like a gag. If it was still alive, it wouldn't be biting or communicating with the others; that was a risk she was not willing to take. As the dead one was pulled up and thrown onto the concrete, it opened its eyes. There was a hard cataract crystallization over its eyes. It was blind. They realized it relied on its sense of sound just like a bat to see. One more mystery uncovered. The group kept quiet, but Joey couldn't contain herself. She was horrified. It cocked its head towards her trying to reveal its razor sharp triangular pointed teeth, but the gag stopped it. The ropes were tied tightly confining it, forcing it to walk with the direction of the ropes. Tamara and Maya took the front while Moose and Elliot took the rear. Loris led the way with Ellie and Joey right behind him. Loris was the most important member of the group now. Getting them back to safety without running into anymore of the dead ones was most important. Their hideout was just a few blocks away, but he knew luck wasn't on their side.

They walked slowly, careful not to step on anything noisy like twigs or other random things on the street; they were just a block away. The figure was lashing out, but it was mostly contained. The ropes were doing their job. They reached the building and just in time.

"Guys, I have a bad feeling about this," Joey muttered.

"What do you mean?" Maya asked.

"It just feels like something is watching us." She kept turning to look back.

"It's just us," Tamara opened the door and they all went inside.

Tamara and Moose placed the dead one in the cage Moose had made, tying the ropes to the others so its limbs were tied behind its back. The puncture wound from the bamboo had miraculously healed itself, bearing no hole or scar.

"Guys, there's no hole anymore...." Maya said, suddenly worrying again.

"Great, so they can heal themselves too. They really are indestructible."

"Don't say that word! We captured one. We WILL find its weakness and then we will destroy it along with the others," Tamara said taking lead. It looked like Maya was no longer in charge, all things considering.

"It's almost light," Elliot said. "What do we do?"

"We get to work," Tamara said handing Moose a tool they would use on the figure.

DAY 28

CHAPTER 17

"**W**hat do you mean...get to work? Are we going to dissect it?" Joey asked horrified.

"What did you expect—give it a cup of tea and ask questions?" Tamara said indifferent. "Now, I suggest those of you who can't handle what comes next, leave."

Joey was the only one who left without further consideration. The others stayed and watched.

"So we know that stabbing them in the head or chest, which would kill a human doesn't work. We know that it can heal itself. What else do we know?" Maya questioned.

"Look at the eyes. They can't see. They rely on their hearing and click just like bats do with echolocation. And they travel in packs," Loris added.

"Anything else?" Elliot prodded.

"The bodies, the victims' bodies disappear after. Loris and I saw them evaporate right before our eyes."

Everyone turned to Ellie and she couldn't tell if it was appreciated information or not.

"Yet another mystery," Elliot said annoyed

"Well that's already more than we knew before. Now, we just have to figure out how to kill one," Maya said.

The next moments were the hardest for them. It felt like torturing an animal, but they knew better. They knew if it were the other way around, the dead one wouldn't hesitate, and they'd all be its next snack. Moose and Tamara prodded the monster, starting from the top, stabbing and waiting for the reaction. Sometimes it jerked in response to the pain and sometimes it was unresponsive.

Ellie looked away unable to bear to see so much oozy blood-liquid spurting out. After about an hour and no step closer to finding out how to kill the thing, something strange happened. It began to disappear right before their eyes. At first, it wasn't so obvious, the teleportation started from the feet and worked its way up the lower body. Ellie was the first to notice.

"Guys, you need to hurry up. It's disappearing!"

"What are you on about?" Tamara said before realizing half of its body had already disappeared into thin air. "Fuck!" she said slamming a tool into its chest cavity and splashing around. It was useless, the sun was coming up and it disappeared right before their eyes.

"Where the fuck did it go?" Tamara screamed, throwing the tool to the ground, she was covered in its blood. Moose kept the same expression he had from the day Loris and Ellie met him.

"It's ok, we did well," Maya said trying to raise group morality.

"We did well?! Good isn't enough! We went through all of that effort and what did we accomplish? Nothing, we're back to where we started," Tamara said storming off, Moose followed behind. Maya rolled her eyes and took a deep breath.

"It's not easy, you know."

"I never implied it was," Ellie said. She had so many questions, and her head was already imploding.

"I thought if we injured it and confined it, it wouldn't be able to leave. But it still found a way. How is that even possible?" Maya asked herself.

"What even is it?" Ellie turned to Loris. "It looked like a zombie-vampire." "I don't know what to believe anymore, but I think after everything that's happened, we have to be open to all possibilities, even the crazy ones.

"Its claws and teeth were so sharp...one cut and it could slice your stomach open..." Ellie said in a panic.

"Let's get something to eat. We're safe for now," Loris said heading to the aisles with all the best sugary and fatty foods.

Ellie obliged. She was starving.

The rest of the day, everyone kept their distance for the most part. Ellie and Loris rested in their room and Tamara and Moose were on the rooftop drinking.

"What now?" Ellie said to Loris feeling defeated.

"We keep trying."

"And what if..."

"We keep trying till we succeed."

"That's one of the things I love most about you—your optimism."

"I'm far from optimistic," he corrected.

"Then why..."

"Someone has to give you hope," he stared into her eyes, being reminded of the kiss the other night. She felt it too. She grabbed his hand and kissed it.

"Thanks for always having my back."

"Anytime."

As nighttime approached, Maya called everyone in for a meeting downstairs.

"Look, I know last night didn't go as we wanted it to, but we still have to keep trying."

"What do you suggest Maya? Capturing them right before dawn

won't give us enough time," Tamara criticized.

"Well, what do you suggest Tamara? You seem to love undermining everything I say or suggest. This isn't the first time you've had an issue with me."

Tension was filling the air, and everyone's bodies tensed up. Maya and Tamara stared intently at each other, waiting for the other to make the first move. Moose and Elliot stood next to Tamara and Joey slowly gravitated to join.

"You too, Joey?" Maya said betrayed. "After everything I've done for all of you!"

Ellie and Loris stood in the middle.

"It's not like that," Joey started. "We appreciate everything you've done but things have changed, and we need someone like Tamara to make the hard decisions." She reached out for Maya's arm but Maya jerked away.

Maya turned to Loris and Ellie and looked at them with pleading eyes.

"And you? I saved you both." Tears filled her eyes.

"We're grateful to you Maya," Ellie started. She wasn't sure why things were escalating so quickly. Everything seemed fine between them earlier.

Maya was clenching her fists and staring at her feet.

"I care about you Maya, we all do, but we need to try a different approach. We've tried your way but we're getting nowhere. How long do you think we can stay here? How long until we run out of food? How long before we run out of options? We need a plan that's sustainable."

"We're doing just fine!" Blood started dripping from her hands. She had dug her nails so deep into her palms. She didn't even notice.

Ellie didn't want to step it, it wasn't her place. She kept quiet which provoked Maya even more. Maya turned towards Ellie and Loris,

"So that's how it is then," Maya said with such intensity in her eyes. "You know..." but before she could finish her sentence, they were interrupted by a banging on the door. They had been in their standoff for so long; no one noticed that night had fallen.

"It's them," Joey said retreating as far away from the door as possible. "The one that disappeared must have led them here. They know where we are! What do we do Tamara?!" Everyone looked to her for answers.

"We hold our ground. They're not kicking us out of our home," she said grabbing some of the tools she used to torture the dead one and started handing them out.

"Don't be ridiculous! They'll kill us all. You saw those things and what they're capable of first hand! Be reasonable!" Maya begged.

"If you're not going to help, you can leave," she said dropping a sharp tool into Maya's hand. She clutched it tightly in fear. Everyone stood by the door, praying it would hold, hoping they wouldn't have to fight. They knew deep down it was a battle lost, but hope and charisma were powerful things, and Tamara would not bend under the pressures that Maya had. She was capable of making the hard choices. While everyone stared at the door, Ellie and Loris' eyes were stuck to each other. She grabbed his hand and clenched it tight.

"Loris, I..."

"I know," he said. He could see what she wanted to say through her eyes. "Me too."

The door held for a while until they broke through. The moment they started swarming in, everyone lost their courage, just like Maya had predicted. It would be a bloodbath. Joey and Elliot were the first to abandon their posts. I guess he had settled for the girl after all. It was better than being alone. They ran towards the stairs. Maya took off right after trying to catch up with them. Tamara turned to Loris and El, "Don't you fucking dare!" But Loris already was dragging Ellie up the stairs to try and hide. They didn't have much time, seconds only to choose their hiding place. As they got upstairs, they opened up a hall closet and closed themselves inside. There was no lock, their silence would determine if they would survive. Ellie couldn't stop panting; it had become her defense mechanism. Loris gave her his hand, and she breathed into it like before. She wanted to look away, but she couldn't keep from staring through the crack between the closet doors.

"Retreat!" Tamara ordered to Moose as they climbed to the top of the stairs. They were still alive surprisingly. One of the dead ones had climbed up the side of the stairs and took Moose by surprise.

"Moose!" Tamara screamed as her loyal comrade fell. The look in his eyes was haunting. He didn't scream but his mouth laid wide open, exposing his cut-off tongue. They never would hear the story behind that. Tamara turned to the other three that focused all their attention on her. She drew her sharpened weapon up and slit her own throat, falling down onto her knees. Every part of Ellie's body was shaking as she watched the blood spurting out like a fountain. Within moments the three figures were on top of her, tearing into her flesh. They gazed through the crack as the monsters mashed and gnarled at her broken body. They watched as the remaining life left her eyes. She looked hollow and devoid of life.

Then screams started coming from above, they were from Joey.

"Elliot! Let me in! They're coming!" She was pounding profusely on the door above. He was unresponsive. Typical Elliot, sacrificing in the name of self-preservation.

"Elliot! Elliot!" she pleaded with one last attempt to get him to unlock the door, but he didn't. Her screams were the loudest of them all. It took her the longest to die. Elliot and Maya were safe for now. The figures rummaged through the area led by the one who was tortured a day ago. They left right before dawn broke. And as they left, Ellie and Loris saw the bodies of Moose and Tamara disappearing as well. They vanished into thin air, but the blood and the carnage was still there.

They stayed in the closet for hours after the figures had left waiting for Elliot or Maya to emerge. Elliot was the first. He walked out from one of the rooms overhead and began his descent.

"Hello?" he called out to check if he was the only one. Ellie and Loris remained quiet. They heard what he had done and wanted to get as far away as possible from him. If he could do that to Joey; someone he had known longer, he wouldn't think twice before doing the same to them if the opportunity arose.

"Elliot!" Maya said ecstatic and out of breath. She was limping. She threw her arms around him and relaxed into his chest. He let her linger there for a moment before pushing her back.

"What happened?" he asked referring to her leg.

"I tripped over something while trying to escape, I'm fine."

"I'm leaving," he said grabbing a bag and throwing in some basic amenities.

"Take me with you," Maya said desperate, hobbling to her bag. He stopped in front of her and grabbed her shoulders and looked into her eyes.

"We both know you'd only slow me down. Take care Maya," he said leaving out the door. Maya collapsed to the floor and started weeping. It was over for her.

Loris and Ellie emerged from the closet after some time and walked to their room and packed up what they could and headed downstairs without speaking a word. Maya turned to look at them, but her eyes were hopeless.

"I don't want to live in a world like this," she said with such calmness now, almost acceptance. Loris noticed the empty pill bottles surrounding her. Maya noticed they saw them.

"Oh, don't worry about me, my pain will be over once and for all soon. It will be on my own terms, not like theirs," she said referring to Joey, Tamara and Moose.

"Maya.." Ellie said going up to her. She grabbed one of the pill bottles and checked the label.

"It's too late for that. I can already feel them dissolving in my stomach. It'd just be a wasted effort. I'd only hold you two back." She was trying to look at Ellie but her eyes were starting to glaze over.

"My vision's already started to get all fuzzy. It won't be long now. And besides, you have each other to worry about."

"What do you…"

Maya shook her head and let out a chuckle, "Oh come on, don't tell me you still don't see it."

"See what?" Ellie asked.

"You're really going to make me say it?" she turned towards Loris' direction. "Just don't wait until it's too late to tell her," she said, her eyes becoming more withdrawn by the minute. "I mean everyone can see it, but you both should just admit it and be honest with each other before it's too late."

Ellie grabbed Maya's hand and sat with her. Maya rested her head on Ellie's lap and Ellie and Loris stayed with her until the light left her eyes and her heart beat for the last time. Loris covered her with a blanket before they left. He grabbed Ellie's hand and they started out the door. There was nothing more they could do for her. Ellie hoped she found peace. At least she got to die on her own terms and not at the hands of the dead ones.

DAY 32

CHAPTER 18

For the next few days, they wandered the streets and stayed in abandoned buildings while making their way to the harbor. They didn't talk much during that time; they were too focused on finding a safe haven. So focused in fact that, by the time they reached the boatyard, they didn't have a clue what to do next.

"They're all gone...." Ellie said disappointed but not surprised. She was getting used to being let down.

Loris wasn't about to give up. "There's some out there," he said pointing to the sea.

"Are you suggesting we swim? With all our gear?" Ellie responded.

"Yea, that's exactly what I'm suggesting," he said.

"Ok." She was determined to find a way off this hellhole.

Loris looked back at her to see if she was really ok with the idea. She was already rolling up her sleeves. He didn't need to convince her.

"Really? You're not gonna try and convince me that this is a bad idea?" he asked surprised.

"Nope, let's do it."

"And what if the boats have no gas or we can't rig any of them to run?" he questioned.

"Then we keep swimming," she said.

Loris laughed in approval.

"You ready?" Loris asked.

Ellie grabbed his hand. "Now I am."

In unison, they jumped together into the murky water. Hong Kong's water wasn't known for its blues or clear visuals. It shouldn't have even been called an ocean. Their bags floated and they pulled them along heading to the nearest boat. Loris helped push Ellie up on the first boat. No luck—the gears and propeller were rusted over; it had been years since this boat had been in commission. The second boat showed more promise; there was no rust but also no key. The optimism was slowly going down as well as the sun.

"I think we have time to make it over to the last boat up ahead," Loris stated.

Ellie looked into the sky and prayed it would be enough time. But she knew that, even if the boat did work, they wouldn't be leaving on it till the morning. Spending a night exposed and vulnerable on the open sea was frightening. She hoped it would be worth it.

"El, come here!" Loris called. He was dangling something in front of him--a pair of keys. "Check this out," he said as he turned them into the ignition and the boat fired instantly, showing an almost full tank of gas. Luck was on their side after all. Ellie hugged Loris immediately in excitement and relief. They were both soaking wet but there was a certain warmth radiating off them.

"It's getting dark, so we'll have to sleep here tonight. Are you ok with that?" he asked.

"Have to be," she said looking around for a place to sleep. There was a small compartment underneath, Ellie was hoping it was the sleeping quarters.

"Should we go check it out?" she asked him.

"I mean, we got time," he joked.

When they opened the compartment, they saw a bunch of fishing equipment but no bed.

"Damn, that sucks."

Loris moved all the fishing equipment to one side and rolled out a tarp onto the floor. He grabbed two sacks for pillows and motioned for Ellie to sit down. He secured the compartment door by placing something in between the hatch lock.

Ellie sat down and tried to relax, but the floor was hard and cold.

"Come here," Loris said.

Ellie leaned against his body and he wrapped his arms around her. "Feel better?"

"Yeah," she said with her eyes closed. "Just wish we didn't have to wait till morning. It's like we're so close but..."

"So far? I know, but we will make it," he said pulling her closer. She felt safe in his arms.

"Should we talk about what you said before when you thought..." Loris asked.

"I mean, I think we both thought we were about to die," Ellie said clarifying. "I don't think what I said really..."

"Fair enough," he said not trying to push. "But Ellie I do-"

She cut him off before he could finish. She wasn't ready to hear those words in a concrete setting. "Let's just get through this night," she said squeezing his hand.

He sighed but agreed.

The night went by quickly. Distant screams and screeches were mostly drowned out by the waves swaying the boat back and forth. It was a familiar comfort.

In the morning, Ellie was covered in her own drool. Loris was watching, waiting for her to realize it. She wasn't as humored. Loris started up the boat and within minutes of the sunrise, they were off. They hadn't even thought of the plan for when they arrived to Lamma Island, both of them had been so fixated on getting there that the thought of what they were going to do hadn't crossed their minds. As they saw Lamma Island approaching, Ellie started asking questions.

"So, what are we going to do once we arrive? What if they've reached the island?" she said suddenly doubting her plans.

"Well first of all, it's broad daylight; the sun is at its highest position in the sky. And secondly, have you no faith? Everything is going to work out, don't you worry," he said pulling her in for a side hug.

She smiled slightly. She had trust in his words.

They pulled into the harbor and docked the boat slightly offshore. They didn't want to risk anyone commandeering their only means of escape off this island. Ellie and Loris grabbed their packs and jumped into the sea, swimming to shore. It was refreshing for both of them. They hadn't felt this free and at peace in a while. Everything seemed, normal, almost. Ellie flipped onto her back and for a moment just floated in the sea, head up and staring blindly at the sun. She let go of all her worries and for a second was back to her old self. As they reached the shallows, Loris started splashing Ellie like a child at play. The salty water got into her mouth, she flipped back over and started splashing back. They got lost in each other's childishness. Their bags had floated to shore, and it was if the whole island had been waiting for them.

"We made it!" Ellie shouted out in joy. She started spinning around. She was ecstatic.

Loris was equally as happy. He grabbed Ellie's hand and squeezed it hard.

She looked at him and smiled. It wouldn't have been possible to make it this far without him. Ellie and Loris took a deep breath and made their way to the shoreline hand-in-hand.

Once they reached the sanded beach, they grabbed their gear and looked around. It was quiet, and there were no people in sight. They weren't sure if they should feel relieved or concerned. It could easily go either way. Ellie took the initiative to walk inland towards the houses.

"Hey, just be careful," Loris said to her.

"Always," Ellie smiled back.

They had reached the first row of houses and shops and all was quiet. The windows weren't boarded up like in the city, and all the shops hadn't been looted. It looked like just another ordinary day in Hong Kong.

"Where is everyone?" Ellie said confused. There was no trace of the figures having reached here. *Where would everyone have gone?* It didn't make sense.

"Maybe they evacuated."

"But why, it's safe here. Whatever is happening in the city isn't here. Why would they leave?"

"I don't know. Let's just keep our eyes open."

As they walked through the rows of houses, something seemed eerie.

"El, I have a bad feeling. I think we should keep moving," Loris said as they approached a house.

Ellie wasn't convinced.

"What do you mean? It's broad daylight. Plus, there's no blood or carnage anywhere. I think we're safe for now." She went to open the nearest door. It was unlocked, and she was met with no resistance. She walked inside and saw a fully stocked kitchen with all of the non-perishables out on the counters and a few liters of water, untouched. But it wasn't the time to be questioning luck, it was the time to take what they could get.

"Loris there's enough food here to last us for months!" Ellie exclaimed. They finally had a win. Loris had his doubts. As Ellie checked out all of the choices between the canned food from pickled beets to baby corn, Loris searched the perimeter to make sure they were safe.

"El, we need to leave," Loris said coming downstairs in a rush. He looked wary.

"What's wrong?" Ellie asked confused.

Loris grabbed her as she was packing up some of the cans and rushed her out of the house.

"What was that about?" Ellie demanded. "There was nothing wrong with that house. It had food and shelter and everything we've been needing."

"Let's just find somewhere else to stay, ok?" he pleaded.

"No, tell me why we can't stay there. I'm, we're exhausted, and we deserve this."

"El just leave it ok?" Loris said but she wasn't having it.

"What's going on? What happened? Loris looked in her eyes and contemplated telling her the truth. It was a truth she simply wasn't ready for.

"What? What did you see? Just tell me," she looked deeper into his eyes, searching for answers.

"It's here, El."

Her expression dropped, and she realized what he meant.

"What did you see?" she kept insisting.

"A family all in bed together with the covers pulled up tight."

Ellie covered her mouth in disbelief.

"They all still had these goofy smiles on their faces like everything was normal. It took me a minute to notice the BBQ grill in the corner and the smell and stench of charcoal on all the linens."

"But why...why would they do that? The dead ones haven't even reached here."

"They obviously knew something we don't. We need to keep moving El," Loris guided her forward.

"We could try another house. I'm sure it was just this one. With our luck, of course we chose the one house with a suicidal family." But she knew that was a lie, the whole village had the smell of charcoal, and it was only becoming apparent to them now.

"We'll be ok," Loris said, reassuring her. "Hey, remember you told me you wanted to find your favorite place on the island? Your secret hideout that no one knows about? How about we find it now?"

"It's so far away though; it must be on the other side of the island. We won't make it by dark."

"Maybe not, but we can try to go there," and in that moment, Ellie started to regain hope.

"Ok, let's just find somewhere to rest tonight," she said.

They ended up sleeping in one of the small shops. Loris thought it would be safer than wandering into a random house and being met with unexpected house guests.

They didn't talk much. Ellie had felt defeated. She thought Lamma Island was the answer. Loris had too, but they each felt they had let the other down.

DAY 33

"Ok! So are you going to show me where this secret hideout of yours is?!" Loris teased.

"I've never shown anyone before, guess you'll be the first," she played.

Loris grinned.

"It's a bit of a hike, but once we reach the train tracks, all we have to do is follow them and it'll take us right there."

"Wait, did you just say train tracks? On Lamma?"

"Ok, so I'm going to nerd out for a minute, but Lamma actually used to have a train system."

"What do you mean? That's crazy."

"So, a long time ago, Lamma had these caves. And they hadn't been explored or exploited yet. And one man, the first explorer, found gold and other worthwhile gems. It wasn't long until he started exporting them and turning a profit, but they were heavy and the distance between the caves and the main roads were long, so they built a train to transport it all."

"So what happened?"

"Well, it wasn't long until they bled the caves dry of all their treasures and there was nothing left. After, it didn't make sense to have a train, and it became forgotten. Eventually nature just reclaimed what was hers to begin with."

"Why is this not in the history books!?" Loris was mind-blown though he wasn't entirely sure if Ellie was serious.

"Who knows? Anyways I stumbled upon them a while ago and just followed them to the end, and came upon my hideout as you call it."

"How'd you find it? Did you trip over the tracks or something?"

Ellie turned red and looked at him confirming the truth.

"Wait, no way!" he said stepping back and trying not to laugh. "You didn't!"

"It's not exactly easy to see them. Let's see who's laughing when you trip over them today!" She pushed him.

Loris pushed back playfully.

They kept walking until Loris discovered the tracks.

"Ok, I may have been a quick to talk; they are truly hidden," he said, trying to regain his composure.

"Mmm hmm...." Ellie walked gracefully passed him.

They started their journey on the tracks.

CHAPTER 19

As the day progressed, they walked for miles, growing tired and weary of ever reaching the end. The railroad tracks extended beyond what their eyes could see. The further they walked, the closer they got to what could potentially be a safe zone but there were no guarantees. They had to keep going, they were exposed out here. There was no shelter or safe place to camp out at in any direction--just open tundra lands that needed serious up keeping.

"You ok?" Ellie said tossing Loris some water.

"Yeah, just would be nice if we could find somewhere to finally rest," he said wiping his brow and taking a sip. "How long do these tracks go for?"

"It shouldn't be much further," she said, but she wasn't entirely sure. It had been a while since she last came here. "What's the first thing you're gonna do when we find somewhere to rest?" Loris asked trying to stay positive, even though he had his doubts.

"I'm going to sleep for a whole day and eat the snickers I've been saving!"

"Thought you were saving that for a special occasion," he said chuckling.

"I would say finding somewhere that the dead ones haven't reached *is* a special occasion," she elbowed him.

"Fair enough."

"I'd even share my snickers with you."

"Wow, that's, well, thanks. I know how much those sugar bars mean to you."

"They do. They really do. What are you going to do, Loris?"

Stopping for a moment, he got deep in thought.

"I'm going to make you happy."

"You're what?" she thought she heard him wrong.

"Once we find a safe place, I'm going to make you happy. The happiest you've ever been."

"What do you mean by *happy*?"

"I mean exactly what I said; there's no other interpretation of my words. It's just whether or not you choose to hear them," he said picking the pace back up.

As night approached, they were guided by the moonlight and thousands of twinkling stars that lit their way. They normally wouldn't have traveled at night, but Lamma still seemed to be safe of dead ones for now. They didn't bother to turn on their flashlights. It felt nice to be disconnected from the lights. That is, until it started raining. It hadn't rained in so long and it wasn't rainy season. There was no warning. One moment the sky was chirping with creatures of the night and the next moment, the waves and vibrations of the torrential rain came, echoing and demanding to be heard. Ellie quickly grabbed the ponchos they picked up from the shop and handed one to Loris. They threw them on but they weren't fast enough. Their bodies had already gotten soaked.

"We need to hurry," Ellie said clutching her bag close, trying to prevent everything from getting wetter.

They began to run, desperate for shelter, for anything they could hide under, but there were no trees in sight. Their vision had become clouded from the storm, only being able to see five feet in front of themselves. They ran as fast as their worn-out legs could carry them, trying to avoid sliding on the slippery ground.

"Loris, I think I see something up ahead!" she said, exhaling the cold air from her lungs. "I swear there's a bunch of tall buildings up ahead!" she said.

Desperate to reach them, she sprinted. She never was a runner, in fact, she had gotten kicked off her school's track team for reasons of poor placement. Although, the track team desperately needed people, she was neither a fast nor long distance runner. They didn't know where to place her. So, after the first practice, her coach kindly told her to maybe not stick with track. She was devastated as she was the first person in the history of the school to be kicked off the track team.

As they got closer, the distant shadows warped into trees, one with a box at the top. A treehouse.

"Loris! Look! A treehouse! We can reach it!" she said not paying attention to her footing. Her foot got stuck between a railing and she was pulled to the ground.

"El!" Loris shouted catching up to her and examining her ankle. It looked bad. But there wasn't time to waste. He grabbed her around the waist and pulled her up, helping her get to what they both hoped to be a safe space.

He placed her against the tree directly below the house, shielding her from the downpour. Wiping off her face with his long sleeves, they both looked up to see what was in fact a tree house. It appeared to be empty too, so luck might just finally be on their side. But they both should have known better.

"We made it," she said smiling at Loris, almost forgetting about her ankle.

"I'm going to check it out first. Wait here," he said examining the tree. He climbed the surprisingly sturdy ladder and made his way up. Looking around, he noticed a shelf full of MRA's, canned food, candles and some classic books. There was a double mattress on the floor missing its cover with two pillows and a fleece blanket. This would do. He brought up all their stuff and threw it in a corner. He would deal with that later.

"How's it look?" Ellie called up.

"You're gonna get to eat that snickers," he shouted back, seeing her flash a smile.

He helped her up the ladder, step by step, giving her one last boost at the top. He wished he could see her face when she first laid eyes on the place; it must have lit right up. He hadn't seen hope like that in a while.

"Do you think someone used to live here?" she said, taking off her poncho and soaked jacket. It was waterproof, but everything had its breaking point.

"Don't know, but it certainly seems like they were prepared for some serious shit," Loris said motioning to the MRAs and other survival gear.

"It's freezing," she said, rubbing her arms up and down when she suddenly noticed a bottle of King Robert's Whisky on the shelf. "Ah, look what we have here," she said cheekily, flashing the bottle at Loris.

"King Roberts? You can't be serious. Don't you remember telling me that it was worse than petrol? You can't be thinking of drinking that."

"Desperate times, and besides don't pretend you haven't drank this before," she said opening the bottle and taking a gulp. She passed it to him. "It'll make you warmer," she said trying to convince him.

"Well, it's not like we have any other options," he said taking a bitter sip. "Mmmm...That's the stuff."

"Haha, I remember we used to drink this stuff all the time when we were too cheap to buy proper drinks at bars. Good old 7-11," she said taking another sip.

"We have that in common. Hey, slow down, are you trying to get drunk?"

"It's not the worst idea. What are you doing anyways?"

"Searching for something to wear. All of our stuff is soaking wet. We need to get out of these clothes or we'll get sick."

She wobbled over to help him. There wasn't much but they did manage to find a long, oversized hoodie and some Nike sweatpants.

"Here, put this on," Loris said handing her the hoodie.

"Thanks. But what about you?"

"I'm alright, these sweats are enough for me," he said.

Ellie started to try and get out of her wet clothes but she squealed in pain.

"Here, let me," Loris said going to help her.

She nodded and began to unbutton them. It wouldn't be weird unless she made it. He grabbed her jeans from her waist and slowly pulled them down, being careful not to get them caught around her ankle as she leaned against the wall. As he knelt down, he looked up at her for a brief moment and saw the scars on her upper thighs. He wanted to kiss them, to make her feel like everything was going to be ok but he knew that would make things weird. She saw him notice and pulled down the hoodie, trying to cover them up. He looked down immediately, getting back up and folding her pants.

"I was going through some pretty dark shit," she said. "I dealt with it the only way I knew how. I haven't done it in years though so don't worry. I'm not gonna start back up."

"I wasn't worried," he said still facing away.

"You just look...disappointed."

"Not disappointed, just surprised."

"Why's that? I'm sure you've met lots of people who've hurt themselves. It's the new trend apparently," she said still repositioning the hoodie, downplaying the severity of it all.

"Surprised that you would do that to yourself is all. You seem to have the world at your feet."

"Don't be ignorant," she said, growing slightly annoyed. *Didn't he know better?*

"I wasn't trying to," he said placing the pants in the corner with all the other wet stuff. He slid into the Nike sweats and took off his shirt. He had gotten so much stronger over the past month, and it showed. Ellie couldn't help but notice. She turned around and removed her bra that was still underneath the hoodie.

"I can't believe we got so lucky," she changed the subject. "I mean what are the odds of finding a place like this?" She climbed into the bed like it was her own.

"Yeah, we really lucked out." He sat at the edge of the bed, his back still facing her. He was so close to the edge, he could have fallen off.

She grabbed the bottle of King Robert's and took another swig, then tossed it to Loris.

"What are we toasting to?" he winced at the smell of the cheap liquor as it touched his lips. It was a smell no one ever got used to.

"To new beginnings," she grinned, sticking out her tongue.

"Cheers to that," he took a large gulp, droplets of whisky escaped from the sides of his mouth.

"Here," she leaned over and wiped the drops from his chin and licked her fingers in a suggestive way. Loris became fixated on her lips and scratched his cheek. *Did she do that intentionally?*

"Sweet," she laughed. She had started to feel the effects of the alcohol. Loris turned slightly red at the turn of events. It was the combination of suggestiveness and the Asian flush. Grabbing the bottle from him, she grew bolder.

"Let's play a game," she said raising the bottle up.

"How about truth or dare" he chimed in.

"Just like before?"

He leered. Ellie flashed back to her childhood briefly. She had her first kiss playing truth or dare. Thomas Barker was the lucky guy, but at the time, Ellie believed she was the lucky one. The most popular boy in school, being dared to kiss her--the chubby and frizzy-haired one with a metal mouth. In any other circumstances, he would never have given her a second glance but here they were.

Ellie, like many young girls imagined her first kiss being one from fairy tales. She would practice with her girlfriends, on her favorite stuffed animal--Pooh Bear and even her hand. She had heard from her sister, hand practice, especially when it came to French kissing, was the closest to the real thing. Boy was she wrong. Ellie's first kiss was all but epic. It was a hormonal disaster that everyone in her school got to witness. She never did quite live it down. Thomas had the reputation of being experienced, so young Ellie believed that he would lead with his tongue but when it came to the kiss, tongues darted everywhere but missed insertion. It looked like two dogs were greeting each other. It was horrendous. And because Thomas didn't want his reputation ruined, he blamed poor little Ellie for being such an awful kisser that even he couldn't work his magic. But instead of remembering this terrible experience for what it was, Ellie felt almost nostalgic. The innocence of it all. She missed that.

"Alright, so Loris, truth or dare? If you choose and then refuse, that's a shot. If I think that you're bullshitting me, that's also a shot, no make that two."

"I don't remember there being so many rules," he chuckled.

"Would you like to add one to make it more fun?"

"If you lie when choosing truth, that's the bottle."

"Ha, but how would you know if I was lying?" she said confidently.

"Do you accept this rule?" he said in a creepy imitation of the antagonist Jigsaw from the early 2000's horror movie *Saw*. His voice was spot on.

"Alright, game on," she said positioning herself closer. "So, truth or dare?"

"Dare."

"You would."

"What does that even mean?" he asked amused.

Rolling her eyes in a playful way, she continued. "I dare you to tell me something you've never told anyone before," her eyes lit up.

"That's your dare? Are you sure?"

"Yup."

"I've always been into older women," he said teasing.

"Oh, come on! Be serious!" she said crossing her arms.

"I answered you," he said sticking out his tongue. "Your turn, truth or dare?" They continued for a while, their dares and truths being all in good fun, but then the mood suddenly changed. It was Ellie's turn.

"Dare." She had chosen an equal combination of truths and dares before. This one would tip the scales.

"I dare you to sing for me," he said, knowing she never did for anyone before. Her whole body became tense and her posture stiffened.

"I told you, I don't sing for anyone. I only ever sing in the shower. Besides, it's not like you really want to hear me, do you? Ask me to do something else."

"So, are you saying no?" he got ready to hand her the bottle. It was still very much full. Too full for Ellie's liking. She was not ready to finish it.

"Ok, but close your eyes. I don't want you to laugh at me."

"Oh, come on, aren't we past that? Don't be so serious."

"Close them!" she said commanding him in her teacher voice.

He closed his eyes, but after a few seconds he couldn't wait anymore. He opened them slightly and saw Ellie facing the wall silently practicing. She was too cute. When she turned around, he closed his eyes quickly, hoping she hadn't noticed him peeking or as she would have termed it *creeping*.

"If you laugh, I will kill you," she said as she put on her game face.

Loris slowly opened his eyes again, realizing she was too focused to notice. It was as if she had something to prove. She started swaying back and forth. Her ankle seemed to be healing up or perhaps the alcohol had made her forget about the pain. She let the mood take over as if she didn't have a care in the world.

"I don't want to hold your hand

I want to kiss your lips

I don't want to be your friend

I want more than this

It's a different type of loneliness

When I say I love you

And you say I love you too

Not I feel the same as you."

She sang, twisting her body and twirling her hair between her fingers. She was so charming without even realizing it.

As she sang the last line, she realized Loris was staring straight at her with admiration in his eyes. She gazed back and everything became silent. They locked eyes for what felt like an eternity before Ellie put too much weight on her ankle and lunged forward.

"Careful," he said catching her. He helped her sit back down. "It's selfish to keep that voice to yourself."

She was at a loss for words. She felt a sudden change inside of herself. She couldn't quite put her finger on what it was or perhaps she knew exactly what she was feeling and was just too much of a coward to admit it. Confessing her feelings to herself was far scarier than anything lurking outside. She was tired of being afraid. She grabbed the bottle and took a sip.

"Thirsty?" he joked.

She smiled without looking up.

"Truth or dare, Loris?" she used his name this time, making it more intimate.

"Dare," he said, he hadn't taken his eyes off her. He was thinking about her choice of lyrics. Did they mean anything more than just words? Were they her words?

Taking a deep breath and calculating how much alcohol was left just in case, she went for it. There was literally nothing left she could lose, or so she thought.

"I dare you to kiss me," she said in a tremulous voice.

Loris was taken aback, clearly not anticipating the dare, and didn't react in the way she had expected.

"You're drunk," he said trying to play it off. He didn't want to take advantage of her.

Ellie immediately regretted her bold actions and misunderstood his response as rejection.

"I'm just kidding!" she said, not convincing anyone, especially herself.

"It's not that I don't..."

Cutting him off, "No, no, no, I'm serious. I didn't mean it. Just let it go, ok? Let's just talk about something else," she said taking the bottle back and taking frequent sips like it was beer. She had this nervousness about her where she always had to have something to do with her hands.

Loris didn't know what to say. He had wanted to kiss her for the longest time and had made it clear on numerous occasions. But it didn't seem right for him to give in now, especially when she was so vulnerable. He didn't think she meant it.

"You're beautiful, El," he said, trying to get her back.

Putting down the bottle, tears started rolling down her cheeks. She couldn't hold it in any longer. They had been building up for so long. She hadn't cried since the whole thing had started. There was no room left in her body for all the water that had compiled. She felt like she was drowning. She needed that release. She felt so confused. So lost. So hurt. So alone. But she wasn't alone.

Loris moved closer towards her and wiped the tears from her eyes with his hand.

She hadn't expected that. She laughed nervously. She felt so embarrassed that she had been rejected again. But she hadn't. She then realized why he wouldn't waste their first kiss on a stupid dare. Without warning, she grabbed his hand and placed it back to her face, brushing her cheek tenderly. His hands were rough and calloused, but they felt how a home should feel. Comfortable and safe. She didn't want to be alone anymore. She leaned into his hand, and grabbed the other, cupping her face so she felt secure. It was just him and her against the world, inside their little treehouse that came to their aid. They were both soaking wet from the torrential rains and were huddled close together to keep warm. Passing the bottle of King Robert's Whisky back and forth, they celebrated this small victory. It had been so long since they could properly rest without interruptions or horrors of the world. The black rain was almost a blessing in disguise. Almost.

He kept watching her intently. Her cheeks had become a warm, flushed red from a combination of having finished off the bottle and crying. She hadn't felt this safe in a long time. She had never cried in front of anyone, including her husband. She never felt safe with him. But she felt safe with Loris. He was always there no matter how hard everything got. She could close her eyes and just hide and forget about all the chaos and wrong in the world. She knew someone was looking out for her.

"I don't want to be alone anymore Loris," she said moving her head from his shoulder to his ear as her cheek brushed against his. She turned slowly to meet his gaze, her hand now circling the side of his face. He looked at her desperately. He wanted to give her everything. They had become constants in each other's lives. Against all odds and formulaic equations, they had found each other. They saw each other like no one had seen another before and understood all the depths and layers of the skin. He would have done anything for her.

"El, wait" he gulped. "I don't want you to regret this later." There was a line. A line that she would regret crossing the next day. A line that she had so firmly and frequently reminded him of before everything went down. She was just lonely he said, he kept trying to convince himself. But he knew based on her actions and everything that had happened, it wasn't true. And she wasn't his teacher anymore, things were different now. They could finally be together fully. The line had been blurred and distorted, it ceased to exist. It only remained in their heads.

"You feel it too, don't you?" she said closing her eyes and reaching for his lips. "I don't want to wait anymore."

He couldn't hold out anymore. He had been strong for both of them for too long. He had wanted this for so long, ever since the day he first saw her, but he knew he shouldn't have these feelings. She knew she shouldn't have these feelings. They both had been fighting it for so long to the point where it made them both physically and mentally sick. He couldn't help it. He had been suppressing his urges for so long that he couldn't stay in control.

He took one last agonizing look at her and all of her perfect imperfections, surrendered, and kissed her.

They forgot just how devastating the world was outside. They explored every part of each other's bodies and let each other in. With his rough hands, he was so gentle with her, but she wasn't so easy to break. She reminded him of that as she placed his hand in between her legs and moaned in pleasure. He stuck his fingers into her sweetest and stickiest parts and made sure to give her the attention she so craved.

"I want you inside of me," she pulled him closer, nails digging deep into the crevices of his back.

He looked into her waterfall eyes, and said something he had never said out loud before to anyone, "I love you, El."

"I love you too," she panted. She took control and got on top and inserted him inside of her. The intensity and moaning grew even louder. But there was no one to hear and even if there was, they didn't care. All that mattered was this moment. Not tomorrow, not the future, but now. They tasted each other's sweet meats and surrendered to each other and their vulnerabilities. If tonight was their last night, they wouldn't have minded.

As they became one, they had found something they never thought they'd find again--hope. A reason to live. Something worth fighting for. They forgot just how devastating the world was outside.

Ellie and Loris fell asleep in each other's arms, naked without a care in the world. She wasn't thinking about right and wrong. She had spent her whole life trying to do the right thing and quite honestly, her life had never felt quite right. It didn't matter that Loris was, or for those technicality people, still her student. He had saved her and had shown her how remarkable she could be in her own skin. He let her shine in a world that was full of smoke clouds. Despite her breakdowns and insecurities, he never gave up on her. He could have left her in that multipurpose room, but he didn't. He could have left her any time after but fought even harder. He was right.

DAY 34

They were both awakened the following morning by a loud crash of thunder. They weren't going anywhere, at least for today. The weather had gotten significantly worse and outside had become one big swimming pool of mud. The train tracks were practically invisible from where they were. Loris rolled over to look out the small window. Nothing was visible outside. Ellie, not sure what to say after last night's events, turned over to her side, clutching the pillow tightly. Loris got back into bed and grabbed Ellie tightly around her waist, pulling himself closer to her. She grabbed his hand, lacing her fingers with his. She didn't have the right words to say so she just closed her eyes and enjoyed the moment.

She didn't want to think anymore. She had been overthinking her whole life from frozen yogurt choices to whether or not she really should renew her gym membership to figuring out what everyone else was thinking. She would stress herself out over all the hypothetical situations that could be running through someone else's head and still end up making terrible life choices. She never realized people were in fact, not that complex.

"Did you sleep well?" Loris asked burying his face into the nape of her neck and shoulder, sniffing her hair. It smelt like strawberries. She nodded her head without saying anything.

"Last night was..."

She turned and kissed him hard before he could over compli-cate things with his words. She was trying to think of what to say but there were still no words. She felt inherently guilty. She shouldn't feel this way and she knew it. She had to let it go somehow.

"Can we just stay in bed all day," she asked, turning back to her original position. Usually lazy days were reserved for weekends but there was no telling what day it was. They stopped keeping track. It seemed pointless and moreover, depressing, especially with the holidays.

"Doesn't look like we're going anywhere today at least," he said referring to the weather. The rain had gotten heavier and the ground had become puddled. "I'll be right back, I'm gonna go..." Ellie nodded before he finished. She knew what he meant. They had gotten used to relieving themselves outside when there wasn't any other option.

As Loris descended down the ladder, Ellie took out her note-book she had been carrying around with her and started recall-ing the events of last night. She wanted to make sense of every-thing.

'You see, the problem with the world is that you realize the things you want, weren't meant to be had. But you crave them. Obsess over them. You make every excuse imaginable to justify your desires. To satiate your inner monster. We're not meant to think logically. You realize but don't realize what you will lose in the process. But despite the risk, you're willing to risk it all on the possibility that it just might turn into something more. So when a stranger becomes a friend and a friend becomes so much more than anything you could have ever imagined. They never let you down. No matter the moun-tains, they plowed ahead. Even the rainiest days, even the worst fuck-ing days, they held your head up high. And though the waves crashed around you both. They didn't let you drown. A life saver but it should have been me. You should have let me drown. Because we've crossed the line and I don't know what that means for me, or even for us.

How can we define what is right from what is wrong? When all the monuments, statues and facilities crumbles, do we still follow a society that has burnt to the ground? What roles do we play, why is it so hard to figure out?'

We all are searching for meaning within ourselves, that we've restricted and ruled out a parallel of lifelines in hopes of fitting in or avoiding loneliness. We're told and we even believe that we have one agenda, one pre-determined destiny to fulfill. Am I attracted to you because of the circumstances or the contrary? Do I want you because I can't have you, or did I overlook you because it was never even a possibility? We'll never know, will we?

"You hungry?" Loris returned. Ellie quickly closed the notebook.

She was starving actually but she wasn't ready to make eye contact with him yet.

She shook her head slightly, but it was like he anticipated her needs. He got up and took a look at the canned foods on the shelf. Spaghetti O's with franks. *Score.* It was a shame there wasn't a stove she thought but as he was scavenging through, looking for a fork or spoon, he uncovered a small butane gas burner. Instead of immediately sharing the news with Ellie, he decided to surprise her. He still felt butterflies in his stomach from the previous night but was trying his best to play it cool. He didn't want to seem overeager.

"Here," he said scooching back into bed. He handed Ellie a bowl of the Spaghetti O's.

Her face lit up in surprise and glee. She had the face of a thousand smiling suns.

"How did you...these are my favorite!" she said putting the soup down and hugging him. She grabbed the soup and took a long sip. "OMG, and it's hot! You're amazing," she said briefly forgetting the awkwardness, staring into his eyes.

He turned a bit red and looked down.

"Thought you'd like it. I found a small burner and there's still a few cans of gas left. We can eat properly for a while," he said, re-assuring her.

They could be comfortable here.

As they finished their bowls they chatted away like old souls and for the next few weeks it was truly like a fairy tale. The weather stayed unpredictable, so they hibernated away, making this little house into a home. They hadn't talked about what had happened; they just embraced it. It was natural. They were no longer bound by the chains society burdened them with. They were equals. They were lovers.

DAY 53

CHAPTER 20

"So, I don't know how to say it, but we've only got enough food left for one or two days," Loris said breaking the news. It was quiet for a while, until Ellie stopped writing in her journal.

"I wish we could stay."

"Me too, but we've pretty much used up all the provisions here."

"I bet we can find an even better place," she said walking towards the entrance. She was absolutely optimistic. The tree house had done her some good. She looked out and could see the weather starting to get better. The fog had pretty much lifted and she could clearly see the tracks again. Her ankle was all better too so that would make the journey on foot much easier.

Loris joined her, wrapping his arms around her waist and pulled her close. He kissed her on the cheek but as soon as he did, she pulled away. Her burdens and insecurities suddenly came crashing down. She felt so heavy with guilt and shame.

"What just happened?" he asked confused.

"I just...I don't know what this...this is," she said referring to them. She couldn't outrun her feelings anymore. She felt so stupid suddenly.

"What do you mean *this*?"

She turned to face him and broke down in tears. She felt so wrong. "We can't be together Loris. This... it doesn't work. I shouldn't have kissed you in the first place. That was my bad, and I was weak. I shouldn't have let any of this happen," she said finally taking responsibility.

But it wasn't hers to take, she hadn't done anything wrong.

"Are you kidding me right now?" he exclaimed in disbelief. "How can you even say that? After everything we've been through, you're gonna say that?" It was the first time he lost his temper with her.

"What else can I say Loris? What we... I did is wrong!" she said burying her face into her hands. "I'm so sorry, I shouldn't have..."

"It doesn't feel wrong. And it isn't. We don't have to justify or explain ourselves to anyone!"

"You know what I mean!"

"But I don't! I fucking don't El. I know you care about me. And you can try to deny it or downplay it any way you like but it doesn't change the fact that you have feelings for me. You feel something!" He pressed her hand to his heart. It was pulsating.

"Of course, I feel something Loris! Isn't it obvious how I feel? That's not the issue! I'm your teacher for God's sake. I shouldn't have let this happen! You were vulnerable, and I took advantage of that."

"I'm not a kid El! And you're not my teacher anymore. You're the reason I'm trying my best to survive."

"What do you even mean by that? Survive?" she said looking up at him conflicted, her face now puffy.

"If it had just been me out here, I would have given up ages ago. But I have something to fight for. Don't you know that, El?" he said taking a step towards her. "Do you think this is ideal for me? It's not ideal for anyone but it happened and I'm not sorry it did. I love..."

"Don't say it," she said cutting him off. "I just need to be alone right now," she grabbed her notebook and climbed down from the tree house. She felt so confused, her mind was fighting her on both ends. She couldn't decipher what was right.

"Where are you going?"

"I just need some air." Ellie had never been good at dealing with uncomfortable situations. At the first sign of struggle, she would bail, but bailing wasn't an option this time.

Climbing down, she headed East on the tracks to explore the area. It was quiet except for the off-beat crickets that filled the air. She didn't know how far she had walked but she was getting tired and was starting to regret taking off like that. She wished she had just gotten into bed and hidden herself in the covers like she usually did.

On the walk, she hadn't seen much. Just more trees and open plains. After a while, she found a railway platform with a seating area and decided to take some rest. She was frustrated that she couldn't remember which way to go to the caves. It hadn't been that long. She was starting to think about what a horrible idea it was. There wasn't any food or homely comforts there—just safety and her initials carved on one of the walls in the caves. What would they do when they got there? Hide out until everything went back to normal? She realized how stupid and delusional she had been. It wasn't the first time.

After a while, she saw Loris approaching. He sat down next to her and looked conflicted about what to say. He had his hands in his pockets and was avoiding eye contact. He also didn't deal with problems or confrontation well.

"What's going on, El?" He took a seat next to her.

"I'm sorry, I'm just having trouble dealing with everything right now. I didn't mean to go off on you."

"Well, if we're being honest, can I ask you something?" Loris said.

Ellie knew what was coming. She was trying to mentally prepare, but it was hopeless.

"Why did you think you had to get drunk to be honest with your feelings? And with me?"

"I'm just not good at dealing with these types of things," she said still looking out into the distance. "You've known how I felt about you though, so you couldn't have been afraid of rejection. What are you so afraid of? That things will go back to normal?"

"Is that what you want?"

"Of course not, how could you even think that? I just want to know what you're thinking!"

"I'm afraid things will change, that we won't fit, that you'll see me for who I really am, and not the fantasy you've been building up in your head over all these months. Do you know how much pressure that is?"

"I do see you El. I see the real you. I'm not some horny teenager who just sees what he wants. You're not a paper doll. I know you. You're afraid to let people in but don't you see we need each other; we need trust and faith and love for this to work."

"I just don't want everything to change. I want to keep this moment with you. I want to stay in this treehouse forever but I'm afraid as time passes, you'll grow bored of me."

"I could never be bored of you, El."

"I know it's stupid, but that's how I think."

"It *is* stupid," he grabbed her hand and brought it to his face and kissed it.

"Is it wrong that I'm kind of glad the world has ended?"

"Not at all, I feel the same," Loris said lacing his fingers with hers.

They spent the next hours just watching the colors in the sky change and the wind swoosh the leaves around like it was putting on an aerial show just for them. They finally had an understanding.

DAY 55

CHAPTER 21

"Alright, you ready?" Loris asked, packing up the rest of his things. They had overstayed their welcome and they were now down to the last of the remaining food. If they were lucky, it'd last them two, three days tops. They had put all their faith in the idea that they would stumble upon something even better that couldn't be far from here. It was a stupid thing to do but people often aren't thinking straight when they're in love.

Ellie nodded. She searched the tree house one last time to see if they missed anything that could come in handy. She took a moment to stare at the bed where they had confessed their feelings for each other. She wished there was a way she could take it with them but settled for grabbing the blanket.

"I'm going to miss this place," Loris said joining her at the foot of the mattress. He kissed her cheek.

"Well, we have this," she flashed the blanket at him, and he smiled with approval.

"So, how far do you think the caves are from here anyways?" Loris asked walking slightly ahead.

"Not sure, but I think as long as we stay on the tracks, we'll be fine."

Ellie knew the caves weren't a solution but she still wanted to go there. She couldn't explain why but she had to see them one last time. She thought she might find some answers there.

"I'm not too worried," he waited for her to catch up, and then wrapped his arm around her. "I'll never get tired of this."

"Me too." She was drunk on infatuation and couldn't stop smiling every time she looked at him. She could get used to this. It didn't even bother her anymore that life as she knew it was over. She was uncertain about the future, but she wasn't afraid to face it, not with Loris by her side.

As night approached, they took shelter in the tall grass by the cove. It would be easier to stay safe there and keep a lookout for potential threats. They hadn't spotted any dead ones here so far, but they weren't about to let their guard down. There were tons of other dangers that were far worse.

Loris started a fire with driftwood he found that had washed up after the storm. Luckily for them, it had dried out and the seaweed wrapped around it made great kindling.

"You're good at that," Ellie said taking a seat next to the fire on a log she had rolled over. It was just big enough for the two of them.

"Do you want me to teach you?" Ellie nodded. "See the trick is you have to be patient. It's all about the setup. If you're lazy, the fire might start quicker, but it'll go out faster. You want to stack the wood like this," he showed her and handed her a short piece.

He motioned for her to place it on top.

"Now, we want to put the seaweed and twigs underneath and light them first."

Ellie followed his instructions carefully and grabbed the lighter from him. She lit the kindling and stepped back.

"The final step is to blow until the flames get bigger."

She got down close to the fire and started to blow.

"Why are you blowing like that?"

"Like what?" she continued.

"In such a sexual way."

"I'm not trying to!"

"I wish you could see yourself right now."

She was about to respond when the fire suddenly expanded to three times its size. The flames shot up madly.

"Just like that?"

"Yeah, just like that," Loris kissed Ellie playfully.

"We make a good team."

"I'd say so."

They opened the last containers of their food and feasted. It was such a clear night that the moon gleamed bright along with the fire. It was nice not needing artificial light to see each other.

"You know what we should do?" Ellie walked towards the sea and opened up her arms. She welcomed the crisp breeze. Loris stood up and started walking towards her, taking off a piece of clothing with each step. He could see where this was heading.

She turned around surprised to see him almost naked. She still got a bit shy every time she saw him. He reached down to help her take off the dress she was wearing and then scooped her up into his arms.

"This really is just like the movies," she said right before he went in for a passionate kiss. And it was up until he got knee high in water and then dropped her in.

Ellie wasn't expecting it, she flailed out like a fish out of water and crashed into the sea. The first thing she saw when she resurfaced was Loris uncontrollably laughing, waiting for her reaction.

"I can't believe you!" she scowled, right before splashing water at him. They soon found themselves in a splash battle and they both played dirty. Loris would wait for the exact moment when Ellie would open her mouth to get some air and then launch his attack. Ellie enjoyed knocking him off his feet and then jumping onto him in the water. They had drifted quite far out and could barely stand now. The water was up to their shoulders. Ellie wrapped herself around Loris to stay afloat and they rocked back and forth with the currents.

"It always feels like I'm living a new life when I'm with you."

"It feels like I'm living for the first time," she replied.

It felt nice that they were on the same page.

They came back to shore, Ellie still wrapped around Loris like a sloth. She refused to let go but he wouldn't have let her anyway. He laid her down on the blanket and joined her.

"Tomorrow we'll find the caves," Loris reassured her.

"But what if..."

"Don't think too much," he said giving her a kiss goodnight. She turned it into something more.

DAY 56

CHAPTER 22

"I think we're getting close," Ellie said. She had started to recognize the foliage they were passing by. They picked up their pace. Neither of them had any idea what they were going to do when they got to the caves, but they could figure that all out later.

"This way," Ellie said, leading them off the tracks onto an overgrown dirt route.

Loris went ahead to make sure the path was safe. It didn't even cross her mind that it might not be. Loris kept walking ahead when he heard a snap. It was already too late. Within seconds, a makeshift spear sprung out and flung right towards and impacted his chest. It took Ellie a moment to realize what had just happened. Loris stood there quietly for a second like he was admiring the view, his fingers twitching before collapsing onto the ground.

"Loris!" Ellie ran to his side and hovered over him. She turned him onto his side to see how bad the damage was. The spear hadn't gone all the way through, but it was deep enough. She couldn't tell how badly he was injured.

"Loris, Loris...." she kept waiting for him to open his eyes, but he didn't.

She had to be strong for both of them, but how could she be strong in a time like this? She needed him to tell her what to do.

She needed him to tell her everything was going to be ok.

"Loris, answer me, open your eyes. You're gonna be ok. Did you hear me? You're gonna be ok!" She shook him, careful not to touch the spear. He responded faintly.

"El..."

"Oh, thank god."

"You have to remove the spear."

"What?"

"You have to take it out. But first, get something to stop the bleeding once it's out."

"I..."

"You're strong El, you can do it."

Without a moment to spare, Ellie grabbed the hoodie out of her bag and got it ready.

"On the count of three," she began to say.

"Just do it!"

She looked at the spear and thought about the best way to remove it. Slow and steady or fast and quick? She had to be decisive. There was no room for second guessing.

She looked at Loris, and he nodded weakly. She took a deep breath and yanked at the spear with both hands. It was wedged in, she would have to pull harder to get it out clean. Loris screamed out in pain.

"El!"

"I'm trying!" she mustered up the rest of her energy and pulled with all her might. Loris' life was depending on it. The spear retreated and Ellie yanked it out and tossed it aside. Blood spurted out like a waterfall. She knew she didn't have much time.

She wrapped the hoodie around his shoulder and tied the

sleeves together, tightening it as much as she could. It's not enough, she thought. It has to be tighter. She kept pulling at the sleeves and finally got it tight enough to stop the bleeding. She held her hands over the wound, applying pressure for the next ten minutes, hoping the blood would stop.

Ellie passed out from exhaustion on top of Loris and woke up hours later. It was going to be dark soon. Loris had passed out from the pain but was now becoming more lucid as well.

"El...."

"Loris, are you ok?" *What a stupid thing to ask. Of course, he isn't ok. He was just impaled with a wooden spear.*

"We need to get out of here...."

"What?"

"Whoever set that trap can't be far from here. We need to move."

"I don't understand..."

"It's no coincidence that trap is here El. Someone set it up here for a reason. And I don't want to wait around to see for what."

Ellie helped Loris up and they headed back towards the tracks. Their pace had slowed down significantly, but they were both glad to be away from whatever they had just walked into.

As they continued, Loris began to grow weaker. He was trying his best to hide his pain from Ellie but it was getting harder with each step. He knew what he had to do in order for her to survive.

"El, I'm not going to make it," he said "Yes, you are, don't say that!"

"I need to sit down. I can't walk anymore." She helped him sit.

"El, you know I'm right. I know you. I know you want me to fight, but I can't. If I fight, I'm going to bring us both down."

She shook her head. She couldn't believe what she was hearing.

"You're not right. We're going to get through this together. There's no point if we can't do it together."

"Do you hear yourself El? I'd never be that selfish as to drag you down with me."

"It's not selfish. You're not forcing me. It's my choice!"

He was getting weaker by the moment. He didn't want this conversation to be the last exchange between them. The last memory she would have of him.

"You still have a chance! I want you to live! You have so much more time ahead of you. Don't let me stop you."

"I don't want to live forever. I want to live with you… now," she said clutching his chest tightly. She was holding his hand and leaning over him, looking for answers.

"El, this doesn't work if you don't let me go. Let me do this for us."

"You mean for you, so you can feel better."

"We had our moment and that's enough. I got to have you. I never imagined I could feel so full of love, and I did. We were happy and that's enough for me. All I ever wanted was to be yours," he said reaching out for her cheek but the distance between them prevented him from doing so.

"You can't just give up. We can make it. I can't do this without you. We're a team."

"El, you're so much stronger than you realize. You're going to survive this, you're going to make it. You're a fighter. You fought for me when I wouldn't. You've fought for everything you believe in, and you're not going to stop now. Not because of this. You have to leave me here. There's still a chance for you."

"You know I won't do that. I can't. All of this is meaningless without you. Do you think I'm going to have this happy new life without you? Don't you get it, I can't. I won't. We came this far! It doesn't just end."

It was useless arguing with her, the only progression was the pools of blood growing around the silhouette of his body. Ellie's pants were soaking most of it up, but they had reached their maximum absorbency. He had been hiding his pain well, but time was running out and he didn't want to waste their last moments together fighting. He knew he couldn't join her, even though he desperately wanted to be by her side. He would have given anything to get it right.

"It wasn't enough, it's never enough," she was manic now, letting her darkest thoughts start to take over. It was only a matter of time until her mind would relapse back to autopilot to help her cope with her loss.

"What's not enough?"

"Love. They always say that love is enough, but it wasn't, and it isn't now. I just thought that we would be the exception." She slumped back and joined Loris on the ground, laying down beside him, careful not to touch the hole in his chest. Her head rested on his shoulder and her clothes further soaked up the puddling blood. She noticed the subtle changes in his body temperature.

Looking up, she admired the sky for what felt like the very first time and thought to herself how she would describe a sunset to someone who didn't have the eyes to see. She felt the weight of everything dissolve as she got hypnotized by the colors and felt herself being lifted up. She forgot where she was and what was happening for a brief moment. She felt like she was floating. She couldn't remember the last time she looked up and saw the pooling hazy lilacs and pinks swirled together like lazy candy floss around the last rays of the sun on the horizon. It felt like eating a boiled sweet: the delicious flavor lasts forever as the treat melts on your tongue. For the first time in her life, Ellie stopped overthinking and worrying. She accepted her reality and decided to live in the moment.

"It's beautiful, isn't it?" She squeezed Loris' hand tighter.

"Yeah, it really is." He couldn't take his eyes off of her. He mustered the last of his strength to kiss her one last time. He wanted her to be able to hold onto that kiss forever. She felt the life leave him as her lips locked with his, but she didn't pull away, she wanted to join him, wherever he was going. This wasn't her world anymore.

She stared up at the sky and watched the vastness of black swallow her up. The spark in her eyes started to dim and the color in her cheeks retreated. She turned to Loris and wrapped his arms around her and burrowed into him further. They became bound by blood. She was just hoping he would wait for her. It wouldn't be long now. She uncovered her wrist that she had been hiding from him. She had made the cut earlier when she realized Loris wasn't going to make it. It was deep enough that she wouldn't have to worry for long. But she didn't worry. She knew everything was going to be fine, better than fine. It would be perfect. They could be together, forever. They could have their happy ending on their own terms. This wasn't their world anymore.

"I'll see you soon," she said as she watched her surroundings become blurred until there was nothing but black.

DAY 63

EPILOGUE

"**S**he's awake, do you want me to bring her to you?" he cupped his voice over the phone to prevent spooking her. She was very fragile. "Noted, Doctor."

The orderly rolled her wheelchair out into the sitting room and approached the door with the plaque that read *Dr. Conners*. He knocked twice before opening the door. The room was dark except for the light escaping through the slits in the newspapers that covered the windows and the dim fluorescent lights that kept flickering on and off. *Why are the windows covered*?

"Thank you, that will be all," Dr. Conners said. She stood up and took a seat on the plastic-sheeted sofa and crossed her legs.

"How are you doing today, El? Are you ready to talk?"

She looked around in fear. *Was this hell*? Loris was nowhere to be seen. She remained silent.

"I said, are you ready to talk about what happened?" Her tone shifted slightly. She wasn't in the mood to play games.

She was suddenly parched and tried reaching out for the glass of water on the table besides Dr. Conners but was yanked back. Both of her arms were confined in a jacket. She became frantic.

"What's going on? Where am I? Why am I here?"

Dr. Conners sighed and grabbed the glass.

"Are you thirsty?" she asked bringing the glass to Ellie's lips.

Ellie turned away. She didn't trust this woman. There was something cold about her. Something off. She couldn't quite put her finger on it. She didn't look like any doctor Ellie had seen before.

"I don't understand," she was at a loss for words. Where was Loris?

"All in due time. You've been through so much already. It's going to take some time for your recovery. Let's start with the basics. What do you remember?"

"Where is he?"

"Who?"

"You know who." Ellie was convinced this woman wasn't here to help her.

"I don't know, so why don't you tell me?" She started to scribble down in her notebook.

"Loris... I need to see him." She tried to stand, but her legs were also strapped to the wheelchair. She was confined.

"Easy. Easy." Dr. Conners stood up and went behind her. Ellie couldn't see what she was doing. "Maybe you just need more time." But before Ellie could protest, she felt a sharp jab in the side of her neck and her vision became blurry. The last thing she saw was the orderly coming back in.

"What did youuuu dooo to me..." she slurred. She felt so tired but was fighting to stay awake.

"Let's try again next week. She's bound to come around," Ellie could hear Dr. Conners talking to the orderly.

"But what about..."

"Next week, let's try again," she cut him off and warned him not to finish his inquiry.

He brought Ellie back to her room and strapped her to the cold, hard bed and left before administering another shot.

"This should keep you quiet," he muttered. He loved seeing her helpless. He thought she had already passed out but she was still conscious even though her eyes were closed.

DAY 70

The following week passed by with no qualms. Ellie remained sedated until her next visit with Dr. Conners. No one bothered to bathe her. They didn't have enough manpower apparently. Everyone was stretched thin as it was. It was hard to find good help nowadays for this type of profession. You might not come in crazy, there were a lot of misdiagnoses and ill-intent in the past but spending decades of your life here would drive anyone insane. Humanity didn't exist within these walls.

The drugs were still wearing off and left Ellie feeling out of it but when she saw the orderly come in, she knew better than to fight.

"Are you ready to talk now, Ellie? Or are you going to be difficult?" Dr. Conners asked as she entered the room.

Ellie nodded. She knew she had to be smarter. She looked at the calendar above Dr. Conners' desk and noticed there were seven new marks on it to cross out the days that had passed. When she first noticed it before, the X was on a Monday and now it was already on Sunday. A whole week had gone by, but it just felt like yesterday that she was here right in this room. What did they give her?

"Yes, I'm ready."

"I'm so glad to hear that, Ellie." Dr. Conners smiled, loosened the restraints on her arms and handed her a glass of water. She was being rewarded for her compliance.

Ellie gulped down the whole glass. She felt like her body was drying out from the inside. Dr. Conners chuckled and poured her another glass.

"The medicine will do that to you. Better stay hydrated."

"Where am I?" Ellie asked looking around. The newspaper covering the windows was still there.

"I'll ask the questions if you don't mind. It's easier that way. Ok?"

Ellie nodded. She didn't want to lose any more time. She had to find Loris. She had to get out of here. Wherever here was.

"Do you know why you're here, Ellie?" Why did she keep saying her name?

Ellie shook her head. Of course, she didn't. She had just asked that question.

"We're here to talk about your relationship with a former student."

Ellie's eyes widened. Loris.

"Is he ok? Where is he? I need to see him!"

"Unfortunately, that won't be possible. He's dead."

So, this wasn't hell. It was even worse. Ellie was alive, and Loris was still dead. It was all coming back to her now. Someone must have spotted her and saved her before she had bled out. She looked down to check her wrist, but Dr. Conners had already tightened the restraints preventing her from moving her hands again.

"I don't understand. Why did you save me? You should have let me die." She started to breakdown.

"Is that what you wanted? To die with him?"

"Of course, it is." Ellie was losing control, but she had to stay focused.

"Tell me about your relationship. When did it first start?"

"Why are you so interested in my relationship with Loris? It's none of your business!"

"Actually, it is. A student died and people are looking for someone to blame. His dad is suing the school for negligence."

"His dad? His dad is dead! Everyone at that school is dead! This doesn't make any sense."

Dr. Conners turned to El, "Is that what you think?"

"I saw them, I saw them all die. It was just us left. Loris, he saved me and...." Ellie was hysterical.

"Saved you from what, El?

"The dead ones, they were coming to get me. I was trapped and Loris he rescued me. We found a boat and we...." Everything was becoming a blur. She couldn't remember suddenly.

"The dead ones? What does that mean, Ellie?"

"The monsters...they..."

"There are no monsters here. You made them up."

"What?"

"There are no monsters, El. They're in your head."

"What? I don't understand? Then why are there newspapers covering the windows?"

Dr. Conners laughed. "Oh that? They're doing construction, and I'd rather not have to look at such an unpleasant view if I can help it. Would you like to have a look?"

Ellie was silent. She was trying to process everything she was told.

"What is the last thing you remember, Ellie?" Dr. Conners came and sat next to her and placed her hand on her shoulder. She felt so cold.

Ellie's mind went straight to lying beside Loris, waiting to join him on the other side.

"I just remember laying on the ground next to Loris."

"At the school…."

"No, it wasn't at the school, it was…"

"We found you at the school with him, El."

"What do you mean? The school? We haven't been back there since this all started."

"What started?"

"The reckoning, the dead ones, whatever the hell those things are. They ravage and tear people apart and then simply disappear."

"El, there's no sort of thing like that. This isn't the end of the world, although it may seem that way to you. Losing someone so close to you can make it feel that way."

"I'm not crazy."

"No one is saying you are. I think you've just been traumatized. It's all too much to take in. Sometimes the brain can't process grief and makes things up, helping us to deal."

"That's not what happened."

"I know you're hurting, but we really do need to know more about your relationship with Loris."

"Why? How is that important?"

"We think it might be why he jumped from the top floor of the school. We're trying to understand why he would do something like that."

Commit suicide?

"He wouldn't do that. He isn't a coward."

"No one is saying that. But we need to understand what happened."

"We didn't do anything wrong." She started to cry. She couldn't be strong without him now. She needed him to tell her everything was going to be ok.

"You are aware that having a relationship with a student isn't allowed and is highly inappropriate right?"

"Yes, but... it's different now. He wasn't my student anymore. I'm not his teacher."

"So you're saying that you did have a romantic relationship with Loris?"

"Yes, we did but only after..."

"What did you say to him on the roof?"

"What?" Her attention shifted.

"A faculty member at your school said he saw you two on the roof arguing just before it happened."

That's not true.

"Were you trying to end things?" Dr. Conners suggested.

"No, I loved him," she let it slip out. "I don't want to live in this world without him. Just let me die!"

"That said faculty member said he saw you two kiss right before Loris jumped. Did you try to stop him?"

"He didn't jump! He was bit!"

"Did you know he was going to do it? Were you thinking this would give you a clean slate? You wouldn't be caught? Were you planning to do it with him but chickened out?"

"No...I told you..."

"It's amazing, the human brain and its ability to manipulate memories and confabulation to deal with guilt. I'm sure you believe everything you're telling me, but I'm here to show you the truth. I want you to see what you've done."

"I haven't done anything. I'm telling you the truth."

"It's time to open your eyes, El. This will help." She took out a neon purple liquid and a syringe and administered a shot. Her eyes dilated and within seconds, memories of the last year of her life started flashing before her eyes, starting with the first time she met Loris which quickly shifted to them sitting on the park bench and her rejecting Loris' advance. But this time, she didn't reject him. She kissed him back. She felt like a passenger. She couldn't close her eyes; she was forced to watch. Flashing forward to her colleague telling her he saw them together and her denying anything had happened. To the multipurpose room where she was trapped. This time though, there were no figures, just the two of them sneaking around. She had told him to meet her there. No one ever went into the multipurpose room, and the windows on the door had been covered with paper. It was the perfect meeting place. The flashback then brought her to when they first made love, but they weren't in a tree house. It was a Love Hotel in Mongkok, and there was a typhoon 8, so the chance of running into anyone was remote. They had stayed there the whole weekend and disconnected from the world. Ellie turned off her phone completely. She wasn't even concerned that it would raise suspicions. Ellie felt her heart breaking through her chest. She didn't understand why she was seeing all of this. It wasn't true; she knew it wasn't. There had to be an explanation for what she was seeing. But before she could think any further, she was on the top floor of the school with Loris. Every flashback brought an array of colors splashed into the background. They were dancing and painting the next scenes. She watched herself chase after a furious Loris. She had never seen him so angry before.

"Loris! Loris! Stop!"

He jerked free from her grasp.

"Leave me alone, El! Leave me the fuck alone!"

"I just want to help!"

He turned around to face her. "Haven't you done enough?" He was filled with rage, but tears were welling in his eyes. He wouldn't let her see him cry.

"I'm sorry!" she pleaded. "Please, let's just talk about this."

"There's nothing to talk about! You made it clear how you felt."

"You know how I feel, Loris!"

"Yeah? Then why'd you break up with me?"

"You know why, Loris. We can't be together. Not now; it's too dangerous. I could..."

"Lose your job? Yeah, you've made it clear that it's more important than us."

"That's not true, and you know it."

"Yeah? Prove it. Kiss me then."

"What?"

"Kiss me right now, right here."

"I can't, we can't."

"That's what I thought." He walked towards the edge and looked out. "You know, I'm not gonna miss this place one bit."

"What are you talking about?"

"I am going to miss you, though, and how you taste like strawberries."

"Loris, stop. We can work this out. Just get away from there."

"You suddenly care now? You didn't seem to care when you decided to end things. Just like that. Don't I even get a say in it?"

"Of course, you do... you know I care. That's not fair."

"Not fair? Are you going to stand here and talk about what's fair? In a fair world El, we'd be together. You wouldn't be doing this to me now."

She grabbed Loris' arm and pulled him back into her. She tried to hug him, but he pushed her off.

"It's ok though, it really is. I get it, I'm fucked up, I don't deserve someone like you, I never did. You'll be better off without me. Just promise me one thing ok? Be happy and remember us."

"Loris... stop talking like that. Someone is going to see. Let's go talk somewhere else."

"Let them see. Let them all see. I want them to see this." He grabbed Ellie and kissed her hard. She resisted at first but gave in finally.

"Kiss me like it's the last time, El."

And she did.

"I love you, El. We'll be together one day."

"I love you, too," she cried.

As she was watching herself, she begged herself to open her eyes. *Don't let him jump! Stop him! Stop him!* She screamed at herself, but she just stood there dumbfounded and within seconds Loris jumped. She saw him look back at her and smile. He wasn't afraid at all.

Ellie gasped for air and tried to move but found herself back in the wheelchair confined.

"Now, doesn't that feel better? Knowing the truth after so long? You must be feeling so confused." Dr. Conners stroked her hair.

"What did you do?" Ellie demanded.

"It's a truth serum," she consoled.

Ellie had so many questions, but the biggest one was how did Dr. Conners know what Ellie saw in her mind? There was no way for her to have known. This wasn't the future. She didn't have any crazy tech lying around her office that she could have used to see what Ellie saw.

"Let's get you a nice bath and clean you up. You've been through so much today. I'm proud of you for starting to accept what you've done." Dr. Conners motioned for the orderly.

Ellie still couldn't believe it. She was at a loss for words. But she was desperate for a bath. She was willing to play along.

The orderly pushed her to the bath chambers that looked all but clean. The white tubs were stained yellow and the drains omitted a funky smell. He turned the water on, and the pipes started rattling. Black liquid spewed out, but after a few seconds the water turned clear. The tiles felt prickly on her bare feet. She wasn't used to it.

The orderly removed her restraints and told her to undress.

"Can you turn around please?"

"Doctor's orders." He kept his eyes glued on her a little too closely.

She decided to get into the tub with her gown on. She wasn't about to let him see her naked. She wouldn't give him the satisfaction.

He grunted, clearly upset that she had outsmarted him.

There were no windows inside the bath chambers, just high vents and ceiling fans that were being overworked. There weren't any mirrors either. Strange.

As Ellie bathed herself with the bar of soap that had been left on the side of the tub, she kept thinking about what she had just seen. Could it be that she was crazy? What was that purple liquid the doctor injected her with that caused her to see all those things? Did it really show her the truth? Had her mind been playing tricks on her? She started to believe it might be true; why else would she be in a mental institution? Where was her husband? He was certainly long gone by now, but she did find it curious that he hadn't come to tell her off himself. She kept trying to remember everything from before she got here, but the harder she tried, the foggier the memories got and the less sure she became. Was she feeling guilty? Did Loris kill himself because of her? She wouldn't have been able to forgive herself for that? It made sense that she would have confabulated all these memories to cope with her guilt and shame. She never would have been able to forgive herself if it were true. She was supposed to protect him. They were supposed to protect each other. She had never been so unsure of anything in her life. *If you can't trust yourself, who can you trust?*

"Hurry up!" The orderly was growing annoyed at how long she was taking. If she had been naked, he likely wouldn't have said one word.

As she ran the bar of soap over her arm, she realized a 4-inch, fresh, pink scar running up the inside of her wrist to her forearm. Her eyes fixated on the spot in obsession for a few seconds. Then she hid her arm beneath the water, afraid the orderly might see what she discovered. If everything Dr. Conners said was true, then why did she have a scar in the exact same place she slit her wrist right before she laid beside Loris?

It was then that she realized three things: she loved Loris and she never would have done anything to hurt him, let alone watch him plunge to his death; second, whatever she was injected with did not show her the truth but showed a truth someone wanted her to believe, meaning that everything she remembered had happened, including the figures so they were still out there; third, she had to escape somehow, but before that, she needed to understand why she was here and what these people wanted with her.

Why did someone do this to her? What did they have to gain? How did these people know about her relationship with Loris? Why did they care? How did they find them? She had so many questions. But it wasn't the time. She had to play along. If she was alive, was it possible Loris could be, too?

"Are you ready?" the orderly asked approaching her.

"Yes, take me to Dr. Conners, please. I'm ready now," she smiled.